What Reviewers Say About

A Love that Leads to Home

"If you love a slow-burn romance where the characters are carefully dancing around each other while being incredibly adorable, this story is for you. It was an emotional read for me, and if you want a good heart-wrenching story, read it."—*Hsinju's Lit Log*

Freedom to Love

"This is a great book. The police drama keeps you enthralled throughout but what I found captivating was the growing affection between the two main characters. Although they are both very different women, you find yourself holding your breath, hoping that they will find a way to be together."—*Lesbian Reading Room*

The Practitioner

"*The Practitioner* by Ronica Black is the angsty sort of romance that I can easily get lost in. I wanted to fill a tub and bathe in all the feelings. Hell, if I had one of those fancy, waterproof Kindles, I just might have."—*Lesbian Review*

"The beginning of this novel captured my attention from the rather luscious description of a pint of Guinness. I cannot tell a lie, I almost immediately wanted to be drinking it. ...The first scene with the practitioner also pulled me in, making me sit up and pay attention to what was happening on the digital page. The relationship was like a low simmering fire, frequently doused by either Johnnie's personal angst, or Elaine's. This book was an overall enjoyable read and one which I would recommend to people wanting characters who practically breathe off the page."—*Library Thing*

Snow Angel

"A beautifully written, passionate and romantic novella."
—*SunsetXCocktail*

"*Snow Angel* is a novella, and it flies by. It draws characters and scenes in large strokes, and it's good fun if you'd like a quick read that's particularly escapist."—*The Lesbrary*

Under Her Wing

"From the start Ronica Black had me. I loved everything about this story, from the emotional intensity to the amazingly hot sex scenes. The emotion between them is so real and tear jerking at times. And the love scenes are phenomenal. I feel I'm raving—but I enjoyed it that much. Highly recommended."—*Kitty Kat's Book Review Blog*

"Emily" in Women of the Dark Streets

"A darkly disturbing brush with questionable magic that leads to an astounding one-eighty-degree turnaround after an apparent attempt at suicide. Mindboggling!"—*Rainbow Book Reviews*

The Seeker

"Stalkers, child kidnappers and murderers all collide in this fast-paced, dual-plotted novel. This is not Black's first novel, and readers can only hope it will not be her last."—*Lambda Literary Review*

"Ronica Black's books just keep getting stronger and stronger. …This is such a tightly written plot-driven novel that readers will find themselves glued to the pages and ignoring phone calls. *The Seeker* is a great read, with an exciting plot, great characters, and great sex."—*Just About Write*

Flesh and Bone—*Lambda Literary Award Finalist*

"Ronica Black handles a traditional range of lesbian fantasies with gusto and sincerity. The reader wants to know these women as well as they come to know each other. When Black's characters ignore their realistic fears to follow their passion, this reader admires their chutzpah and cheers them on. …These stories make good bedtime reading, and could lead to sweet dreams. Read them and see."—*Erotica Revealed*

Chasing Love

"Ronica Black's writing is fluid, and lots of dialogue makes this a fast read. If you like steamy erotica with intense sexual situations, you'll like *Chasing Love*."—*Queer Magazine Online*

Hearts Aflame

"Sleek storytelling and terrific characters are the backbone of Ronica Black's third and best novel, *Hearts Aflame*. Prepare to hop on for an emotional ride with this thrilling story of love in the outback. …Along with the romance of Krista and Rae, the secondary storylines such as Krista's fear of horses and an uncle suffering from Alzheimer's are told with depth and warmth. Black also draws in the reader by utilizing the weather as a metaphor for the sexual and emotional tension in all the storylines. Wonderful storytelling and rich characterization make this a high recommendation."—*Lambda Literary Review*

"*Hearts Aflame* takes the reader on the rough and tumble ride of the cattle drive. Heat, flood, and a sexual pervert are all part of the adventure. Heat also appears between Krista and Rae. The twists and turns of the plot engage the reader all the way to the satisfying conclusion."—*Just About Write*

"I like the author's writing style and she tells a good story. I was drawn in quickly and didn't lose interest at all. Black paints a great picture with her words and I was able to feel like I was sitting around the camp fire with the characters."—*C-Spot Reviews*

Wild Abandon—*Lambda Literary Award Finalist*

"Black is a master at teasing the reader with her use of domination and desire. Black's first novel, *In Too Deep*, was a finalist for a 2005 Lammy. …With *Wild Abandon*, the author continues her winning ways, writing like a seasoned pro. This is one romance I will not soon forget."—*Books to Watch Out For*

"This sequel to Ronica Black's debut novel, *In Too Deep*, is an electrifying thriller. The author's development as a fine storyteller shines with this tightly written story. …[The mystery] keeps the story charged—never unraveling or leading us to a predictable conclusion. More than once I gasped in surprise at the dark and twisted paths this book took."—*Curve*

"Ronica Black, author of *In Too Deep*, has given her fans another fast paced novel of romance and danger. As previously, Black develops her characters fully, complete with their quirks and flaws. She is also skilled at allowing her characters to grow, and to find their way out of psychic holes. If you enjoy complex characters and passionate sex scenes, you'll love *Wild Abandon*."—*MegaScene*

"Black has managed to create two very sensual and compelling women. The backstory is intriguing, original, and quite well-developed. Yet, it doesn't detract from the primary premise of the novel—it is a sexually-charged romance about two very different and guarded women. Black carries the reader along at such a rapid pace that the rise and fall of each climactic moment successfully creates that suspension of disbelief which the reader seeks."—*Midwest Book Review*

"Ronica Black has proven once again that she is an awesome storyteller with her new romance, *Wild Abandon*. With her second published novel, she has crafted an erotic, sensual and well-paced tale. …Black is a master at teasing the reader with her use of domination and desire. Emotions pour endlessly from the pages, moving the plot forward at a pace that never slows or gets dull. But Black doesn't stop there. She is intent on giving the reader more. *Wild Abandon* hints at a plot twist early on, and while we know who it involves, we do not know what will happen, and how, until the last minute, effectively keeping us spellbound."—*Just About Write*

In Too Deep—*Lambda Literary Award Finalist*

"Ronica Black's debut novel *In Too Deep* has everything from nonstop action and intriguing well developed characters to steamy erotic love scenes. From the opening scenes where Black plunges the reader headfirst into the story to the explosive unexpected ending, *In Too Deep* has what it takes to rise to the top. Black has a winner with *In Too Deep*, one that will keep the reader turning the pages until the very last one."—*Independent Gay Writer*

"…an exciting, page turning read, full of mystery, sex, and suspense."—*MegaScene*

"…a challenging murder mystery—sections of this mixed-genre novel are hot, hot, hot. Black juggles the assorted elements of her first book with assured pacing and estimable panache."
—*Q Syndicate*

"Black's characterization is skillful, and the sexual chemistry surrounding the three major characters is palpable and definitely hot-hot-hot…if you're looking for a solid read with ample amounts of eroticism and a red herring or two you're sure to find *In Too Deep* a satisfying read."—*L Word Literature*

"Ronica Black's debut novel, *In Too Deep*, is the outstanding first effort of a gifted writer who has a promising career ahead of her. Black shows extraordinary command in weaving a thoroughly engrossing tale around multi-faceted characters, intricate action and character-driven plots and subplots, sizzling sex that jumps off the page and stimulates libidos effortlessly, amidst brilliant storytelling. A clever mystery writer, Black has the reader guessing until the end."—*Midwest Book Review*

"Every time the reader has a handle on what's happening, Black throws in a curve, successfully devising a good mystery. The romance and sex add a special gift to the package rounding out the story for a totally satisfying read."—*Just About Write*

Visit us at www.boldstrokesbooks.com

WATCHING OVER HER

by

Ronica Black

2022

WATCHING OVER HER

ISBN 13: 978-1-63679-100-5

This Trade Paperback Original Is Published By
Bold Strokes Books, Inc.
P.O. Box 249
Valley Falls, NY 12185

First Edition: February 2022

CREDITS
Editor: Cindy Cresap
Production Design: Susan Ramundo
Cover Design By Jeanine Henning

Acknowledgments

Thank you to Bold Strokes Books for continuing to publish my work. It's been a wonderful journey and I can't thank you enough!

This book takes place on a fictional mountain in Flagstaff, Arizona. The real Spruce Mountain is located in Prescott, Arizona. But for purposes of the book (and weather), I kindly moved it to Flagstaff.

Prologue

There was no movement from the house.

He lit a cigarette and sucked in hard, grateful for once to be in his own car so he could smoke. He held the fumes in as long as he could, then exhaled, excitement racing through him.

The chill in the air was fogging up his windows and screwing up his view. He ran the wipers, but it did no good. He had to lean forward and wipe the dew from inside the windshield in order to see.

There. That was better.

But still no movement from the house.

He checked the dash clock. It was ten after seven. She was running late.

She was usually out the door at seven sharp if not a little before. But not today. What was different about today?

He inhaled on his cigarette and squinted toward the house across the street. He thought back to the night before. The typical lights had been on, as was the television. Then everything had shut off at ten thirty as it usually did. Nothing out of the ordinary.

He squinted harder behind the exhalation of smoke.

There was one thing different. He hadn't actually seen her arrive and go into the house. Could that've been his mistake?

He was usually there when she arrived home, but last night he'd had to work late. He couldn't get out of it.

Damn her. His boss. He hated that bitch and hated more that he had to answer to her. She'd fucked up his plans and his routine. And now this. No movement.

He considered climbing from the car to walk past the house. See if he could, what? Hear something? Make out some movement inside? Too risky. She could emerge at any second and spot him. No, he couldn't do that. Maybe if he were walking a dog or something he could. But as it was he was dressed in dress slacks and a tie, all set for work. He'd look odd just walking down the sidewalk for no apparent reason.

Damn it.

Note to self.

Get a little dog.

He reached for his small notepad and scribbled the reminder. A dog would serve several purposes. They made people feel at ease and comfortable. It would make him seem approachable and like he belonged. After all, a guy who had a dog had to be an okay guy, right?

He looked back to the house and scribbled some more.

Seven fifteen and no movement.

He checked his previous notes, flipped back the pages. Every single morning, she emerged at seven for her daily run. Every single one. Except for today.

She's gone. She took off. You lost her.

Shit.

He shook the thought from his head and rubbed his freshly shaved jaw.

What to do. What to do.

She *had* caught on to him. He'd purposely made sure of that when she'd first realized she was being watched. He'd toyed with her then. Left little hints that only she'd notice. Fucked with her. Frightened her.

And the more fearful she became the more excited he got. He couldn't stop. Couldn't get enough. It was just too much fun. Seeing her squirm. Watching her freak the fuck out.

She'd tried to fight back. She'd changed her Wi-Fi password, then her Wi-Fi altogether. Changed her phone number. Changed her email addresses, mail key and passwords to her bank accounts and everything else she considered important. But nothing had stopped him. Wi-Fi was too easy to break into with the right equipment, and once he was in there, bingo. He had access to everything she did.

Her phone. He chuckled. Cloning phones was difficult, no lie. But she'd made it all too easy by leaving her phone on his desk when she'd gone to the restroom. And now he heard every word she said, read everything she texted. When her phone rang, so did his. It was just too easy.

As talented as he was, however, it still wasn't helping now, because there was still no movement from the house.

What to do.

It was pushing seven thirty. He had to be at work by eight. And it was looking like he'd have to go without getting his morning fix.

The notion gnawed at his gut. He had to see her. In person. Had to.

He stubbed out his cigarette and lowered his window for some fresh air, suddenly feeling stifled.

He inhaled and started his vehicle, time running out. He had to go.

He drove past the house and accelerated quickly, tires squealing on the turn around the corner.

He didn't get to see her.

Where was she?

What the fuck was going on?

Had she finally outsmarted him?

He grinned as he turned onto the main road.

If she had, there was one thing for certain.

It wouldn't last long.

CHAPTER ONE

The November air was a cool, crisp fifty-eight degrees as Riley pulled into the parking space, inched up her window, and put her Toyota 4Runner into park. She clapped her hands together and turned to look in the back seat.

"Who's ready for marshmallows?"

"I am, I am!" Phoenix declared as he threw his little hand in the air.

Keira, Phoenix's mother, laughed from the passenger seat. "You're going to spoil him rotten."

"Not to mention load him up on sugar so he doesn't sleep tonight," Elise, Phoenix's other mother, said from the back seat.

"He's four," Riley said. "What kid doesn't want s'mores on a chilly night in the wilderness?"

"He doesn't even know what a s'more is," Elise said, opening the back door from her position next to Phoenix.

"Sure he does," Riley said, exiting herself. She closed the door behind her.

"You mean he does now," Elise said with a smirk. "Thanks to you." She leaned in to unbuckle Phoenix from his booster seat as Keira rounded the vehicle to join them.

"It's okay," she said as she slung an arm around Riley. "When he starts bouncing off the walls tonight, you can be the one to stay up with him."

Riley laughed. "You say that like it's a punishment." Truth was she absolutely adored Phoenix and loved spending time with him. And their last two trips to the cabin had been too warm for a fire, so she hadn't mentioned s'mores to Phoenix until now. At the very least she'd been smart enough to hold off until they could actually make some.

"Say that after spending twenty-four-seven, seven days a week with him."

Elise helped Phoenix from the SUV and he immediately bolted for Riley and grabbed her hand. "Let's go, Riley Robinson!"

He loved calling her by her full name and it always made Riley smile.

"Okay, dude, you got it." She locked the 4Runner and the four of them made their way into the large grocery store to load up on supplies before heading up to Riley's cabin on Spruce Mountain in Northern Arizona, just outside of Flagstaff. And number one on that supply list were marshmallows for Phoenix to roast and make s'mores with. He'd done nothing but talk about it the whole drive up from Phoenix, the city he was named after.

He swung Riley's hand as they entered the market. "Where are they?"

Riley studied the signs as Keira and Elise retrieved a grocery cart.

"Over here, buddy." She led the way to the marshmallows while Keira and Elise went another direction to fetch the supplies on their list. They were no doubt enjoying some alone time, even if it would be for only a few minutes. They were, according to Keira, desperate for some time alone. Riley hoped to give them some this weekend as she planned on taking Phoenix for ATV rides to explore around the cabin. He was always fascinated by the tiny horned toads and wild turkeys and other wildlife they'd most likely encounter. In fact, she wasn't sure who was more excited about those upcoming adventures, her or Phoenix. She just hoped the snow held out long enough for her to be able to take him.

Phoenix continued to swing her hand as they rounded the corner to the appropriate aisle. Riley was smiling down at him when she suddenly collided with someone. Taking a step back and blinking, she realized it was a woman who had been coming the opposite direction.

Startled, Riley first made sure Phoenix was okay and then knelt to help the woman pick up her goods. "I'm so sorry," she said.

"No, it was my fault. Should've been paying more attention." The woman's voice was soft but hurried, as were her hands as she scooped up her granola bars and bottles of water. When she stood, she appeared just as discombobulated as she sounded, with food and bottles of water strewn across her midsection somehow being held in place by her arms.

"Here, let me help you," Riley said, taking two things that looked to be ready to fall.

"No, it's okay, I got it." But a bottle of water fell to the floor as she said it. Phoenix promptly scooped it up.

"Here you go," he said.

"Uh, thank you," she said, trying to free a hand to grab it.

"Wait right here," Riley said. "I'll be right back. Come on, Phoenix." She took him by the hand and they hurried back to the doors. Then they returned to the woman who was trying her best to walk while holding everything together.

"Here you go," Riley said, holding out a handheld shopping basket. She carefully took the items she could from the woman and placed them inside. The woman then did the same, dumping the goods into the basket. She took it from Riley and smiled ever so briefly.

"Thanks."

"Sure."

"No problemo," Phoenix said proudly.

Riley tousled his blond hair.

"He's learning Spanish in preschool."

"Oh, that's…impressive," the woman said. Though she seemed to be a little less distressed now, she still seemed to be nervous. Her amber eyes had depths that left Riley riveted, curious at what lay beneath. It took a purposeful strength to tear her gaze away from them to study the rest of her. She had on dark denim pants, hiking boots with thick-looking socks, and a heavy-looking sweater covered by a large jacket. On her back was a full hiking pack. It was crisp outside, but not anywhere close to freezing. The woman, for whatever reason, was overdressed, and from what it seemed, nearly overpacked.

Riley subconsciously smoothed her hands over her own cable-knit sweater and worn jeans. It was too warm for her to need her jacket. Even Phoenix had left his in the car, his moms opting to let him go inside with just his long-sleeved shirt and jeans on.

So the question was, why was the woman so overdressed? And more importantly, why did she look so nervous? And why was she trying to shop for all that with no basket or cart?

The woman grazed her hand over her loosely bound hair, almost like she'd forgotten she'd put it in a ponytail. She played with the loose end, twirling the chestnut locks. To some, it would seem a calm, soothing gesture. With the woman however, it came off as a nervous one. Like she didn't know what else to do with her hand. Her gaze flitted from Riley down to Phoenix and then back to Riley.

"Thanks again," she said.

"Sure," Riley offered.

The woman smiled a smile as fleeting as her gaze and then side-stepped around them. She then disappeared around the corner.

"She was pretty," Phoenix said as he once again tugged on her hand to lead them farther down the aisle.

"Um, yeah," she said, unsure what to say. "She was." She was rather pretty. Striking actually with those eyes and creamy skin. And her lips weren't bad either. A natural mauve with a beautiful, near-perfect shape.

"Can she come make s'mores with us?" Phoenix asked, bounding ahead.

"Uh, no, bud, she can't."

"Why not?" he asked, looking back at her over his shoulder.

"Because we don't know her and because she's going home to her own family."

"Oh."

Riley stopped and gently pulled him back. She pointed at the marshmallows.

"This is it, Phee. These are the marshmallows."

She picked up a bag and handed it to him. His big green eyes widened.

"Wow!"

"See how soft and smushy they are?"

He nodded vigorously as he squeezed the bag.

Riley grabbed a couple more bags and led the way back down the aisle. They headed off to find Keira and Elise.

She thought the whole mysterious woman thing had been left well behind them. But Phoenix surprised her by bringing her up again.

"If the woman doesn't go home to her family, can she come roast marshmallows with us then?"

Riley glanced at him. He was looking up at her expectantly, little hands gripping his bag of marshmallows tight.

"Sure, bud. If she doesn't go home to her family, she can make s'mores with us."

She winked at him and he grinned. Then he ran ahead to show his mothers his prize.

Chapter Two

They spent close to an hour in the grocery store, getting what they needed and then exploring the home goods to pick out things for the cabin. The cabin was a recent purchase for Riley; she'd bought it close to six months ago and she was still in the process of making it feel more like her own. Keira and Elise were happy to help in that department, and they picked out some decorative pieces for fall, along with some cloth placemats and matching cloth napkins. And Phoenix eagerly chose a ceramic turkey as a centerpiece. All in all, they had made a good haul and the sun was close to setting as they headed toward the mountain.

They were laughing and singing when they pulled off the main road and onto the trail that led up to Spruce Mountain. Phoenix was belting out his favorite song, "Cake by the Ocean," the edited version of course, as Riley shifted the SUV into four-wheel drive. Then they began their ascent.

"Can we have cake tonight?" Phoenix asked, apparently more than a little moved by his favorite song.

"Now that's one thing we didn't get," Elise said. "Cake."

"I think that's the *only* thing we didn't get," Kiera added. "We pretty much bought out the store."

"Aw, no cake?" Phoenix said.

Riley looked at him in the rearview mirror. "No cake, Phee. But we have s'mores, remember? And popcorn."

"Popcorn!" He smiled.

Riley refocused on the road and drove them around several bends. It was about a twenty-minute drive up the trail to the cabin, and darkness was creeping in on them as they headed up.

"I wanna see Bigfoot," Phoenix blurted out, the music now switched off.

Elise cracked up and Keira turned in her seat. "Where did you hear about Bigfoot, Phee?"

"At school. My friend Alejandro told me all about him."

"What did he tell you?" Elise asked.

Phoenix filled them in. "He said he's this big, tall, hairy man who lives in the forest and has big feet. And he smells real bad. And he doesn't like for people to see him cuz he's real shy."

Riley tried not to laugh.

"That's pretty close to the truth," Elise said.

Keira shrugged. "It is."

"Can we see him?" Phoenix asked. He was already craning his neck to look out the window.

"I don't know if we'll get to see him," Riley said. "Since he's so shy."

"Maybe we could tell him about the s'mores," Phoenix said. "Maybe he'll come for those."

"Maybe," Keira said. "Everybody loves s'mores. Even Bigfoot."

Riley smiled and then squinted as she caught sight of something ahead in her headlights. For a split second, the talk of Bigfoot registered and her heart leapt. But then as the figure came into view, she could make out a person, a woman, walking on the side of the trail with a large pack on her back. She turned and shaded her brow at the headlights and then hurried off trail into the brush.

Riley slowed, confused.

"Who is that?" Elise asked.

"I don't know," Riley said.

"Who would be walking this trail?" Keira asked.

"I don't know," Riley said. She'd never seen anyone hiking up the trail before. Riding ATVs, yes. On a leisurely walk on the ascent? Not so much. And this appeared to be more than just a leisurely walk. The woman was walking in the brush, her pack weighing her down. As Riley inched closer and recognition sank in, her heart didn't leap, it fell to her stomach.

"Riley, look! It's the pretty woman!" Phoenix was pointing and shouting.

"I see, bud. I see." But the woman seemed to be heading for the cover of the woods.

"Who's the pretty woman, Riley?" Elise asked.

"Someone we met at the grocery store."

Someone I am very surprised to see here.

Riley pulled alongside the woman and eased down her window. She shouted, hoping to reach her before she was swallowed up by the woods. "Hi!"

The woman turned slightly, then fully. She came closer, obviously just as surprised to see Riley.

"Hi." She was breathless and sweating as she approached, even though the temperature was dropping. She ran her hand over her hair again, still seeming nervous. Her eyes even darting behind Riley's vehicle, as if she were checking for more oncoming cars.

"You okay?" Riley asked. *Why were you headed for the forest?*

"Me? Yeah, fine. I'm good."

"I'd offer you a ride, but we're packed full."

"No, I'm good. I got it."

"You sure? I can come back and pick you up after we unload."

"Riley," Elise whispered.

"No, that's okay." Again, her eyes flitted behind Riley's SUV. "I better get going. Thanks for the offer."

"Okay," Riley said, though she didn't feel good about leaving her. Didn't feel good at all. She smiled softly at her and the woman waved as Riley slowly drove away.

"What are you, crazy?" Elise asked from the back seat. "Inviting a stranger into the car with my son?"

"She's not stranger danger, Mama. She's the pretty woman from the grocery store," Phoenix said.

Elise groaned.

"He has a point," Riley said.

Elise hit the back of her seat.

"Seriously, Riley, do you know her?" Keira asked.

"No. Like I said we just met her at the grocery store."

"What's she doing up here?" Elise asked.

Riley shrugged. *I wish I knew.* "I guess she's headed up, same as we are."

"Without a car?" Keira asked.

Riley glanced over at her. "I guess so." She looked in her rearview mirror and saw the woman disappear as they rounded another bend.

"Wonder where she's staying," Keira asked softly.

"I don't know. I hope nowhere near us," Elise said.

"She's alone," Keira said. "Strange."

"Is she going to her family?" Phoenix asked.

"I don't know, bud," Riley said.

"I'm sure she is, sweetie," Elise said.

"Cuz if she's not, she gets to have s'mores with us. Riley said so."

Keira looked over at her and Riley felt her face burn.

"I'm sure Mama's right," Keira said. "I'm sure she's going to her family."

That seemed to satisfy Phoenix because he was quiet the rest of the way, eagerly staring out the window for Bigfoot, while Riley's mind was back with the woman on the trail. The mysterious woman walking all alone up a mountain, destination unknown.

The very pretty woman she'd met at the grocery store.

Chapter Three

*W*izard of Oz, Wizard of Oz!" Phoenix shouted as Riley unlocked the back door to the cabin to allow him to run through. He made a beeline for the couch before she could even find the light switch. When she did, she saw him all settled in the corner of the sofa, hands in his lap, little feet kicking in the air. He was waiting politely for her to put in his favorite cabin movie. *The Wizard of Oz.*

It was a routine they'd come to appreciate. Phoenix would immediately settle in with the Wizard while the rest of them unloaded all the goods. It worked out great for everyone.

Riley set some grocery bags on the kitchen table and then made her way to Phoenix in the living room. Phoenix was on the only sofa while a large, comfy chair sat across from it, just to the side of the big stone fireplace. Riley knelt in front of the old television nestled in the corner and slid in the VHS tape of the Wizard. She promptly fast-forwarded through the storm scene, which frightened Phoenix, and stopped the tape at just the right moment, when Dorothy's house first lands.

"There you go," she said as she stood. Phoenix giggled and clapped.

"Thanks, Riley."

She tousled his hair and took a handful of bags from Elise as she lightly kicked open the closed door.

"That door still isn't sticking," Elise said.

"I know. You still have to push on it really hard to get the lock to engage. Just one more thing I have to fix around here."

"You'll get to it. Give it time. At least it actually locks."

"True."

"He all settled in?" she asked, looking to Phoenix.

"Uh-huh," Riley said as she unloaded her haul on the table.

Elise smiled like only a mother could at her child. "He's so beautiful, isn't he?"

Riley smiled with her, touched her on the shoulder, and then walked back outside to get more goods from the SUV. Keira passed her as she headed for the cabin.

"You put the movie on already?"

"Yep."

She smirked. "Glad we figured out that little trick."

"Works great until the flying monkeys."

"He'll be passed out long before then," she said, walking up the steps to the deck.

"Think so? What about the s'mores?"

She glanced back at her. "You better hurry with those if you want him to partake."

Riley quickly grabbed what she could from the 4Runner and headed back inside. Elise was busy unpacking everything and putting all the perishables in the fridge, while Keira and Riley finished bringing what remained in. Soon they were mostly unpacked and ready to settle in for the evening. Elise even had the coffee maker going, and Riley suddenly longed for a nice hot cup. She slipped into a thick flannel shirt and hugged herself as she crossed to the fireplace.

"I'm cold, Riley," Phoenix said.

"Not for long, bud. I'm building a fire."

"Can I help?"

"Sure."

Riley placed two logs in the fireplace and promptly began unfolding the nearby stacks of newsprint. She handed bits to

Phoenix and told him he could either wad them up or twist them. He chose to twist them before shoving them beneath the logs.

"I think we're good for now," Riley said.

Phoenix stepped back and brushed his hands together. "Me too." He rested his hands on his hips.

Riley sat on the hearth and lit the papers with her stick lighter.

"Know what, Phee? We need some pine cones. Grab me a couple?"

He hurried over to the basket in the corner and plucked out a handful of pine cones. He walked very carefully back to her, making sure he didn't drop any.

"Good job," she said as she took them from him.

She tossed them into the growing fire and then pulled him close to watch the fire evolve with her.

"It's getting warmer," he said, holding out his palms.

"Mm-hm. Soon we'll all be toasty."

His face crinkled. "Like toast?"

She laughed. "Something like that."

"Ew, I don't want to be like toast."

"You don't want to be warm?"

"Not like that."

She stood. "You ready for s'mores?"

He bounced. "Yes!"

Riley thumbed down the volume on the Wizard and then went to retrieve some coat hangers. When she returned she busied herself straitening them out, making a smaller one for Phoenix to handle. Then she caught the bag of marshmallows Keira tossed to her and she and Phoenix settled near the fire.

"Okay, first rule of s'more making. You can only make s'mores if one of us is watching you. Got it?"

He nodded.

"You don't play anywhere near the fire, unless we are with you."

He nodded again.

"Okay, second rule. You're not allowed to make a better s'more than me."

He cocked his head. "Huh?"

She laughed. "Nothing, I was kidding."

Elise and Keira joined them, first handing Riley a cup of coffee and then settling together on the couch. Riley sipped her coffee, groaned at how good it was, and then set it down away from the fire. Next, she opened the bag of marshmallows and handed one to Phoenix.

"Now, take your marshmallow like this," she said as she demonstrated. "And slide it on your stick like this."

Phoenix curled his tongue up over his top lip as he did so. "'Kay," he said as he finished.

"Now, carefully hold your marshmallow near the flames like this."

Phoenix did as she said, his gaze intently focused.

"Good. Now turn it over so you get the other side." Phoenix did and soon she was showing him how to carefully remove the marshmallow to make a s'more, Elise right there assisting. Phoenix loved it and bounced up and down, chewing his first bite. He wanted to make more, and Elise allowed him one more before leading him off for a bath before bed.

Riley pulled her shirt tighter and headed out on the vast deck, looking down into the valley of dark forest and then up into the black star-spangled sky. She leaned on the railing and breathed in the fresh, cold air. She heard someone approach behind her.

"Thought you might could use this," Keira said, handing her her coffee.

"Ah, thanks." She'd reheated it for her. "You read my mind." She took a few sips and allowed it to warm her throughout.

"Whatcha doin' out here?" Keira asked, leaning on the rail next to her.

"Just thinking."

"Thinking 'bout what?"

Riley hesitated to tell her, but Keira seemed to pick up on it. "Not the woman."

Riley bowed her head.

"Riley, no."

"It's near freezing out here, Keir."

"And I'm sure she's in a cabin somewhere all snuggled up next to a fire."

"We can't be sure of that. I mean I think she had a tent rolled up on her pack. What if she's in a tent?"

"She's not. She'd only come up here if she had a home to stay in. This isn't a camping area. Right?"

Riley sighed. "Right."

"Besides, if she'd wanted help she would've asked for it. You offered her a ride. She wasn't interested."

"I know. But something about it…doesn't feel right."

"Then that means you should forget her. If it doesn't feel right then something is probably wrong. And you should stay far away."

"Think so?"

"I know so." Keira wrapped an arm around her and pulled her close. "Now let's get back inside before we freeze our asses off out here."

They hurried back inside and Riley turned to look out at the valley one last time before she closed the door. She hoped with all she had that the woman was okay, somewhere warm and safe. Just like she was.

Chapter Four

Riley rose early the next morning and slowly walked down the spiral staircase from her loft. The living room was empty, as was the kitchen. It seemed her friends were still asleep in their room down the hall. She quietly turned on the coffee maker and got busy making breakfast. Phoenix liked waffles; they were his go-to breakfast at the cabin. Mainly because Riley had a Mickey Mouse shaped waffle maker from when she was a kid. Phoenix loved it.

She put on some turkey bacon for Keira and diced some vegetables for omelets. The bacon was just starting to smell good when Phoenix came ambling in rubbing his eyes. He had on his dinosaur pajamas with matching T. rex slippers. They growled when you squeezed the ears.

"Morning, sunshine," Riley said, whisking the batter for his waffles.

"Good morning, Riley."

He crawled up on a stool and rested his elbows on the counter. His hair was mussed and sticking up in the back. His eyes were barely open.

"Are you making my Mickey waffles for me?"

"Sure am."

He managed to smile.

"Want some juice?"

He nodded.

Keira was the next one to emerge from the hall. She looked snug in a fleece bath robe and husky dog slippers. They also made noise when you squeezed the ears. They'd been a Christmas gift from Phoenix who proudly howled like a husky every time he squeezed the ears.

"Phee, let's go potty and wash up for breakfast."

Phoenix groaned but slid off the stool to follow her into the bathroom. He still had trouble remembering to take the time to use the restroom, so they had to remind him frequently.

They both looked a bit brighter when they returned to the kitchen, with Keira pouring herself some coffee and Phoenix climbing back up on the stool to drink his juice. They'd all started in on breakfast before Elise came in, hair mussed, rubbing her eyes, much like her son had done not long before.

"Why didn't you guys wake me?" she asked.

"We wanted you to get some rest," Keira said, rising to kiss her. She made her a cup of coffee and handed it to her.

"Mm, thanks, babe." She joined Phoenix and Riley at the table while Keira made her a plate. Keira often spoiled Elise when they came up to the cabin, since she was the one who mostly stayed home with Phoenix and cared for him nearly twenty-four-seven. Keira was good about taking the time to pamper her a little.

They ate breakfast while chatting softly, mostly about the day's plans. Keira and Elise were planning on a long walk and relaxing around the cabin while Phoenix set in on begging Riley for a morning ATV ride.

"It's too cold for that," Elise said.

"No, it's not," Phoenix argued.

"We'll go when it warms up a little, Phee," Riley said. "In a couple of hours. Okay?"

He nodded and continued eating his waffles.

"In the meantime, you can help me with those paint by numbers we brought," Keira said. "Remember you brought one that looks like a big tiger?"

"Yeah!" he said.

"Let's finish up with breakfast first." Keira winked at Elise. "That'll give you time to start in on that new book you brought."

Elise held her hand. "Thank you, love."

"Don't mention it."

"What are you going to do, Riley?" Keira asked.

Riley stood and gathered their plates. "I need to chop some wood and check on the ATV."

She carried the plates to the sink and began washing up. Elise joined her and covered her hand in hers. "You cooked. Let us clean."

Riley thought about arguing but then decided against it. She knew she'd lose.

Instead she nodded and slid into her lightweight jacket and gloves and headed down to the basement where the ATV was kept. She flicked on the lights and opened the garage door that had a view of the underside of the deck. The basement was cold and smelled of wood and gasoline. A strange comfort of sorts. She kept the stacks of chopped wood inside against the wall to protect them from rain and snow. Another stack was just outside under a tarp, and that's where she started. She broke down those bigger pieces with the axe and then carried them inside to stack. It was hard work, but she enjoyed it and soon she'd worked up a sweat. She slid out of her jacket and continued, chopping for close to two hours. When she called it quits, her arms were shaking and she had a hard time carrying the wood up the stairs to the living room. Thankfully, Elise saw her and followed her back down to help carry more.

"Thanks," Riley said as they carried up the last needed batch to fill the shelves next to the fireplace. She wanted to be prepared for the snowstorm that was due to arrive soon.

"You're welcome, you lumberjack, you. I don't know why you don't let us help you do things like that." Keira and Elise knew better than to try to help her do any work outdoors. The work was a nice change from her job as creative director at a local software development firm, so she insisted on doing it herself.

"I like doing it," she said. "Makes me feel good. Alive."

Elise just smiled. "You know, you're going to make someone very happy one day."

Riley rolled her eyes. "Yeah, right."

"No, I mean it. You will."

"We'll see." She hadn't dated in close to a year; her last breakup left a rather sour taste in her mouth. Elise knew as much and usually was pretty good about leaving her be about it. Riley was thankful, wanting to come to terms with her breakup and subsequent dating on her own. Trouble was, she wasn't really doing either. She just preferred to not think about it.

"Did you fuel up the ATV?" Elise asked as Riley started to head back down the stairs again.

"Just getting ready to, why?"

Elise smiled. "Because you've got an eager little guy up here ready to go."

Riley gave a thumbs up, knowing that Phoenix wasn't the only one eager. Elise and Keira were no doubt chomping at the bit for a taste of some alone time.

"Suit him up and send him down."

Chapter Five

F aster, Riley, faster!" Phoenix yelled as they accelerated after a turn. Riley pressed on the gas and raced up the trail away from the cabin. Dust and gravel kicked up behind them, and Riley's face was going numb from the chill. They'd been riding for close to twenty minutes, putting ample distance between them and the cabin, climbing Spruce Mountain, bypassing only two other homes. Most of the cabins were lower on the mountain. Riley's was one of the only ones up this high. She liked it that way and enjoyed the solitude and the peace and tranquility.

"Faster!" he yelled again. But Riley was nearly frozen, and she needed to make sure the speed demon wasn't as well. She slowed and eased off the trail at a clearing and killed the engine.

"Why did we stop?" he asked, turning his helmet-covered head. The tips of his cheeks were ruddy from the cold, the rest of him unseen due to the covering of the lower half of his face. Keira had bound him up tightly in his heavy jacket, gloves, and scarf. The boy could hardly move sitting in front of Riley and she wondered briefly how in the world he could even breathe.

She tugged on his scarf and checked the rest of his face. His skin was cold, but he looked fine. And his grin spoke volumes.

"Are you having fun?" she asked him.

"Yes!" He raised a tiny fist in the air. "But why did we stop?"

"I needed to make sure you were warm enough and... I thought this would be a good place for our picnic."

"Yeah!" She helped him down and then climbed off herself. She unloaded the carrying case on the back and handed Phoenix the blanket. "You want to spread that out for us?"

He nodded and she helped him remove his helmet and gloves.

He promptly spread out the blanket and they sat and dug into their lunch of homemade sandwiches and juice boxes. Phoenix ate quietly and slurped at his straw. His hair shone in the sunshine.

"I like it up here," he said. "It smells good."

"Does it?" She took a bite of her peanut butter and jelly sandwich. "What's it smell like?"

"Like trees!"

"Mm, yeah it does doesn't it?"

"Uh-huh. Like Christmas trees."

He took another bite of his sandwich and stared beyond Riley. Suddenly, his eyes grew big and he bolted to a stand. "Look, Riley! It's the grocery store lady!"

Riley turned and saw the woman from the grocery store walking up on them slowly, hands in her back pockets. She was smiling softly, as if not to offend.

"Hi," she said.

"Hi!" Phoenix said, sprinting to her.

"Phee, wait!"

But he already had his arms wrapped around her, looking up at her with his big eyes.

Riley stood and approached awkwardly. "Sorry, he gets a little excited."

"It's okay," she said, brushing back his hair.

"You wanna have lunch with us?"

"Phoenix—"

"We have extra PB and J and even an extra drink."

"Phoenix—"

"I better not," she said, eyeing Riley as if she understood her hesitance.

"Why not?" Phoenix backed away, shoulders slumped. He walked to Riley and wrapped an arm around her, obviously sad.

"She probably has somewhere to go," Riley said.

"Where? She's on a mountain."

He had a point. And Riley noticed that she didn't have her pack or any of her supplies. She realized she must be staying somewhere close by.

"You doing okay?" Riley asked.

"Mm-hm."

"Staying somewhere close?" Riley tried to think of another home up this way, but she couldn't.

"Close by, yes."

Phoenix released Riley and started wandering around, mostly kicking rocks.

"Do you have all you need?" Riley asked, noticing she was wearing the same thing she had on the day before.

"I'm okay."

"You sure? Because—"

"I'm fine."

Riley closed her mouth.

"Riley, come here!"

Riley turned, suddenly realizing that Phoenix was nowhere to be seen. Frantic, she followed his voice down into a nearby ravine. The woman called after her and Riley slammed to a stop as she saw the blue tent erected amongst the trees. Phoenix had found the woman's campsite.

Riley flushed, knowing the woman hadn't wanted them to find it. She felt embarrassed for her and turned slowly.

"It's just temporary," the woman said as she came down and began absently tidying up. "I won't be here long."

"Your secret's safe with me," Riley said, trying to make her feel more comfortable. "But it must be cold."

"It is," she said. "But I'm making do."

"Don't you freeze?" Phoenix asked. "Like a snowman?"

"Not quite," she said.

His eyes grew bigger. "Did you see Bigfoot?"

"Bigfoot?" She laughed. "No, haven't seen him yet."

"Dang," Phoenix said. "I can't wait to see him."

Riley watched the woman closely, still captivated by her eyes. She had a million questions but no polite way to ask them. What was she doing up there? Why was she camping out? Why was she alone?

Phoenix broke the silence by walking up and grabbing the woman's hand. "Come eat with us," he said. "I'll even give you my juice box." He led them back up to the picnic area and the woman helplessly sat down next to him. Riley followed suit.

"Where's all your family?" Phoenix asked, handing her a juice box and a cellophane-wrapped sandwich.

The woman seemed surprised and at a loss. Riley thought about coming to her rescue, but she was more than curious herself.

"I—they're—back in Phoenix."

"How come?" He smacked his lips as he ate.

"Er—because they wanted to stay home."

"Instead of coming up here? Why? It's neat up here. And Riley Robinson says it's even gonna snow."

"Riley Robinson?"

"Uh, that's me," Riley said. "He likes to use my full name sometimes."

"Oh." She studied Riley for a moment, like she too was somewhat curious about her, then her gaze went back to Phoenix as she finally took a bite of her sandwich.

"Do you have a girlfriend?" Phoenix asked, causing Riley to swallow her drink wrong. She coughed and held up a hand to let them know she was okay.

"Phee, that's kind of a personal question," she managed to say. But damn if she wasn't dying to know herself.

Phoenix merely shrugged.

Surprisingly, the woman answered. "No, I don't have a girlfriend."

He took another bite. "Neither does Riley Robinson. But my moms say it's because she doesn't want one."

"Oh," the woman said, this time flushing a little herself.

Riley rubbed her brow wondering what else was going to come from Phoenix's mouth.

"What's your name?" he asked. "Mine's Phoenix and this is—"

"Riley Robinson," the woman finished for him. She held out her hand and shook both of theirs. "Hi, I'm Zoe," she said.

"Zoe," Phoenix said as if trying it on in his mouth. He nodded. "I like it."

She smiled.

"I like Phoenix too."

"Thanks. My moms named me after Phoenix, Arizona, where we live. You know where that is? It's down the mountain past the Walmart. It gets real hot there."

Zoe laughed. "Yes, I know where it is. Remember that's where my family is."

"Oh, right. I don't think Bigfoot lives there, cuz it's too hot and there aren't enough trees."

"Ah."

"He'd have to swim a lot. Do you swim? I do. I take lessons. I can swim under water and everything."

"I do swim," she said.

"Riley does too. She used to be a lifeguard."

"Oh."

Phoenix stood and brushed off his pants to rid himself of the crumbs.

"Can I look for toads, Riley?"

"Sure."

He walked away, eyes peeled to the ground.

"Stay where you can see me," she said.

"'Kay."

"He's quite the young man," Zoe said.

"You have no idea."

She chuckled. "I think I've got some idea."

"Yeah, sorry about all the questions."

"He's just curious. I can understand that."

Riley brought her knees up to her chest. Zoe looked away toward the sunlight and her eyes lit up like light shining through a bottle of whiskey.

"You sure you're okay up here, all alone?" Riley asked softly.

Zoe didn't look at her, just kept staring out toward the sun.

"If I said no, what would you do?"

Riley blinked, surprised. "I guess I'd offer to help."

"How?" She finally looked at her, and the pain Riley saw in her face nearly left her breathless.

"I'd offer you help, food, shelter."

"And if I said that wouldn't help, then what?"

"I—don't know."

She looked away again.

"You can't help," she said. "No one can."

Chapter Six

Zoe hugged herself against the afternoon chill as she watched Riley and Phoenix ride away from her on their ATV. They'd stayed close to an hour, doing their best to politely gather information from her. Phoenix was more direct and playfully curious, while Riley was careful in how she approached the personal questions. Zoe knew she was dying to ask her everything, but Riley held fast to her manners and only asked what she deemed appropriate or what she believed Zoe would be comfortable enough to share. Which really wasn't much, not after Zoe had confessed that she couldn't be helped.

In the end, Riley seemed sullen and almost hesitant to leave her. Phoenix, on the other hand, begged her to come for s'mores. She'd politely declined, but he wouldn't hear of it. Finally, she'd conceded and told him she might be able to stop by. He seemed pleased with that and declared he was going to go back to the cabin and get everything ready for her. Riley had only smiled softly in response, as if she knew better than to try to stop him.

The duo had left her with spirits lifted a little, but now she had to worry about whether or not to show up for the s'mores. There would undoubtedly be more questions, especially from Riley's companions. She'd already sensed their uneasiness when Riley had stopped alongside the road to talk to her. She completely understood their hesitance in befriending her. She was a stranger after all. And one who was camping out in the middle of nowhere on her own. If she were them, she'd be cautious too.

She sat on the nearby log she'd been using as a chair and loosened her ponytail to run her hands through her hair. It would probably be best if she stayed away. Best for everyone. Even Phoenix. Even if he didn't know it. She smiled as she thought of the little guy and his feisty little fire for life. His attitude was infectious, and she'd found herself laughing more than a few times during their visit. But a warm fire indoors did sound nice. As did a nice hot cup of coffee or tea or whatever they may have. It did sound tempting. And Phoenix would be thrilled if she came.

And then there was Riley. Her stomach flipped as she recalled the angular structure of her face, the dark hair, and the blazing green of her eyes. She was an incredibly attractive woman and someone who would be difficult to put from her mind. Just the way she looked at her stirred her. Like she was the most important person on the face of the earth. No one had ever looked at her like that before. The woman seemed to really care, and she seemed truly upset when Zoe had told her she couldn't help her.

Zoe sighed, elbows on knees, fingers entwined in her hair. It had been a little over twenty-four hours since she'd left and already she was craving a shower. Boy, did she have a long way to go. She eyed her watch and looked toward the sun. Nightfall would be upon her before she knew it. She had to try to find the cabin once again. She stood and grabbed her backpack and slung it over her shoulders. She headed for the trail and began the trek upward.

She had four hours till sundown. Surely she could find it before then.

Surely she would find it before she had to spend another night in the tent.

Surely she would find it so he wouldn't find her.

Chapter Seven

W hat do you mean you're sure she won't come?" Elise
asked, following Riley around the interior of the cabin.
Riley continued clearing the table from their dinner. "I mean
she seemed hesitant, guarded even. I doubt very much that she'll
come." In fact, she'd be surprised if she ever saw her again given
how she behaved. Zoe was definitely hiding something and that
something, Riley feared, was not good.

"But you still invited her?" Elise asked as she joined Riley
at the sink to help clean up.

"Phoenix did. And what was I supposed to do? Take it back?
How rude would that have been?"

"Yes! You take it back. You say, I'm sorry, he's just a little
kid and unable to make such decisions. Who cares if it's rude.
We're talking about our safety here."

Riley scraped a plate and then rinsed it before plunging it
into the sink of hot, soapy water. She stared out the window at
the 4Runner and the trail beyond. She considered telling Elise
that everything would be fine, that the woman was no danger, but
Riley couldn't bring herself to do it. Because she honestly didn't
know whether she was or wasn't. Based on what she'd said, that
nobody could help her, Riley would have to say that yes, there
may be something bad going on. But looking into her eyes and
seeing how she was with Phoenix…Riley found it hard to believe

that Zoe would be dangerous. Her gut told her she wasn't. But her gut also told her to be careful.

"I wouldn't worry about it," Riley said, more to herself than to Elise. "I'm sure she won't come."

Elise sighed. "I hope you're right."

"Riley's always right," Keira said, smacking Elise on the bottom as she brought them more dishes. "And Riley's not supposed to be cleaning up. House rules."

Riley continued washing, her gaze lost out the window.

"She won't let me do it," Elise said.

Riley felt a firm nudge to her left. Keira had bumped her out of the way.

"Gotta be aggressive, Mama," Keira said with a wink.

Riley groaned and dried her hands. "Fine. You two have at it."

She went into the living room where Phoenix was sitting on his knees at the coffee table doing a puzzle. She sat on the couch to watch.

"What's this one of?" she asked.

Phoenix stared down at the pieces, fully concentrating. He pointed to the box lid without looking over at it. "The planets."

"Cool."

"Yeah."

Riley stood and crossed to the fire. She poked at the logs and then tossed another one in. The sun had just gone down and the temperature was already dropping. Once again, her mind went to Zoe. While she knew it was unlikely that she would come, she couldn't help but find that she wanted her to.

What was that all about?

She tried to tell herself if was just out of concern for her safety and well-being, but she knew it was more than that. Her interest went beyond curiosity. She was attracted to her.

She rubbed her forehead, not exactly comfortable with the revelation. Thank God it was unlikely that she'd show. Out of sight, out of mind. She hoped.

"Yeah, right," she said softly.

"Huh?" Phoenix was looking at her.

"Nothing."

"Is it time for s'mores yet?"

"Finish your puzzle first."

He nodded like he was agreeing to a very serious mission and refocused on the puzzle. Riley slid into her jacket and headed outside to think.

The air bit into her and she thought of that flimsy tent Zoe was staying in.

"I've got to get her out of my mind."

But she couldn't. She knew Zoe didn't have much. She knew that just by seeing her backpack the day before. There's no way she had everything she needed to keep warm.

I should take her some blankets. And some food. I should do it tomorrow. On my own. I can't just let her sleep out in the cold like this.

Riley turned as she heard someone walking toward the deck. She couldn't make out who it was until they climbed the three steps to join her.

"Zoe?"

"Hi." She was standing with her hands in her coat pockets, breath coming out in mists. Riley couldn't see her face very well in the dim light, but she knew her cheeks must be red from the cold.

"Hi." Riley shook her head in disbelief. "I didn't think you'd come."

"Oh. I can go." She started to back away.

"No, no, no. That's not what I meant." Riley took a step toward her, afraid she would leave. "I meant…I didn't think you'd want to come. You didn't sound very excited at the invitation."

"I just didn't want to disappoint Phoenix in case I couldn't make it."

Riley sank her own hands into her coat pockets, the chill growing stronger.

"He'll be thrilled you did." She offered her a smile. "I'm glad too."

Zoe looked down at her feet as if she were a bit embarrassed. "Thanks."

"Would you like to come in?"

She nodded. "Sorry I didn't go to the front door, but I saw you out here from the trail and thought I'd just come around back."

"No need to apologize. We don't ever use the front door anyway." She opened the back door and motioned for Zoe to enter before her. Zoe did and Riley followed, closing the door behind them. The heat of the cabin enveloped them, and Riley slid out of her coat.

"Look who decided to join us," she said as she hung her coat and offered to take Zoe's.

"Zoe!" Phoenix bolted from the coffee table and threw himself in her arms for a tight hug. "You're here!"

She laughed softly, obviously a little overwhelmed at his enthusiastic greeting.

"I decided those s'mores you mentioned sounded too good to pass up."

He bounced with excitement. "Yeah, they're soo good. You won't believe it."

Riley welcomed her in farther and motioned toward the living room. Keira and Elise joined them from the kitchen, having been watching quietly as Phoenix greeted her.

"Hi," Keira said, approaching with her hand outstretched. "I'm Keira and this is my wife, Elise."

Zoe shook her hand while Elise said hello and settled for a polite wave of the hand.

"We're glad you could make it," Keira said. They rounded the couch and encouraged Zoe to sit. Phoenix made a beeline for the armrest next to her.

"I'm doing a puzzle," he said. "Wanna help me finish so we can do the s'mores?"

"Sure." She edged to the end of the couch and examined the puzzle. "Wow, you've done a great job so far," she said.

Phoenix sat on his knees and started moving pieces around again. Elise took the opportunity to question Zoe.

"So, Zoe, how are you liking Spruce Mountain?"

Zoe glanced over at her but then refocused on the puzzle quickly.

"It's great. I really like it up here."

"Have you been here before?"

She shifted some in her seat before answering. "I came up here as a kid. Stayed with my grandfather."

"Oh, so he has a place then?"

Riley looked at her, curious herself. Zoe appeared uneasy, but she handed Phoenix a puzzle piece and answered nonetheless.

"He—did yes."

"Did?" Elise asked. "Does he not have it anymore?"

Zoe cleared her throat. "He passed away some time ago."

"We're sorry to hear that," Keira said softly.

"Does that mean he died?" Phoenix asked.

"Yes, it does," Keira said.

"That's sad," he said and went back to his puzzle.

Riley studied Zoe closely and noted her thin face and arms and the dark circles below her eyes. She looked frail and exhausted, somewhat different than she had just a day before. But then again Riley hadn't seen her out of her coat. Riley decided to ask her the question that was probably on everyone's mind.

"Is his place still here?"

Zoe looked over at her with eyes wide with what could only be alarm. And for a few long seconds, Riley wondered if she was going to up and leave.

Chapter Eight

Zoe sat frozen, thinking about bolting for the door. She'd been expecting questions, personal ones even, but this, this was too much. She locked eyes with Riley knowing she'd shared too much information already. She couldn't give this away too.

Riley's gaze softened and she gave her a look of what could only be understanding. She slapped her hands on her thighs and stood.

"How 'bout those s'mores?"

Phoenix hopped to his feet and jumped up and down. "Yeah, yeah, yeah!"

Riley held out her hand to him. "Come on, let's go get 'em."

They rounded the couch behind Zoe and disappeared into the adjacent kitchen. She could hear them moving about, opening and closing cabinets, Phoenix giggling every now and then. She was very much aware of the women sitting next to her, but she wasn't sure what to say, the tension still hanging in the air from the unanswered question.

So she sat staring into the fire in the cozy living room, trying to enjoy the atmosphere of the nice cabin, ringing her hands in the process. The cabin was an A-frame in design with a kitchen and dining area directly to the right of the back entry and a living room with a stone fireplace directly to the left. A spiral staircase stood at the far wall adjacent from the couch and led up to what she assumed was another room. The additional rooms were probably located down the dim hallway past the kitchen. All in all, it was a very nice cabin, well kept, with old-fashioned furniture, wood floors, and vaulted ceilings. The view out the large windows to the back patio must be spectacular in the daylight. She closed her eyes, wishing she had such warmth and comfort.

"Can I get you something to drink, Zoe?" Keira asked. Zoe found her smiling softly at her. "Something to help warm you up?"

Zoe thought about declining but then decided to take her up on her offer. Maybe agreeing to the drink would help relax them all.

"That would be great, thank you."

Keira looked to her wife. "What about you, hon? You up for some hot chocolate?"

"Your special hot chocolate?"

"The one and only."

"In that case, yes, please."

Keira kissed her on the forehead and stood. "Zoe, you should know that I spike my hot chocolate with butterscotch schnapps. That okay with you?"

Zoe smiled. "Sure, sounds good."

Keira returned the smile and left them. Elise fixed her gaze on Zoe. "It must be cold staying in that tent."

"It is." Zoe felt uneasy under her stare, like a child about to be admonished by the principal.

"Why are you doing it then? Why not stay someplace warm?"

Zoe opened her mouth to speak, but Phoenix came bounding into the room with bags of marshmallows in his hands.

"Ta-da! I got the marshmallows!" He held them up victoriously.

Riley was right behind him, carrying chocolate and graham crackers.

She looked at Zoe. "You doing okay?"

Zoe nodded.

"Care to join us?" Riley motioned toward the fireplace. Zoe stood and joined Phoenix, sitting in front of the hearth. The heat from the fire felt so good she nearly melted where she sat.

"Feels so good," she said, closing her eyes.

"Here." She opened her eyes after being nudged by Phoenix who was handing her a long wire. She thanked him and noticed that Riley was staring at her as if transfixed.

"You know I've got a lot of extra sweatshirts and blankets you can have." She took a marshmallow from Phoenix and slid it onto the wire then handed the wire over to him. He took it eagerly and held the marshmallow over the flames.

"Not too far in, bud, or they'll burn," Riley said softly.

Phoenix backed away and curled his tongue up to his lip in concentration.

Zoe considered Riley's offer. It was obvious she was trying to help, but Zoe didn't want things to get too comfortable between them. She was freezing at night though. Really freezing.

"I'll think about it," she said.

Riley smiled. "Please do. I'm really worried about you sleeping out there like that."

Zoe's heart panged. "You are?" It was out before she could stop herself.

"Of course. How could I not be?"

"I don't know," Zoe said, shaking her head. "You don't even know me."

"I know enough," Riley said, her eyes softening like they had just moments before. "I know enough to know that I should be concerned."

Zoe held her gaze for a long moment, moved by her apparent empathy for her. Her powerful green-eyed gaze and the sentiment both left her speechless.

"Do your marshmallow," Phoenix said, nudging her again. He rotated his over the fire.

Zoe readied her marshmallow and joined Phoenix. They roasted in silence until the marshmallows were ready and then smiled and laughed as Phoenix did his best to show her how to make a s'more. They ate the first ones quickly, with Phoenix managing to get chocolate all over his hands and mouth. Riley was quick with napkins, wiping him down gently before readying another marshmallow for him.

Keira brought her her drink and Zoe sat back, sitting this roast out and just enjoyed the heavenly spiked hot chocolate. She watched Phoenix and Riley together, observing how easy they were with each other. Phoenix seemed to really love her and vice versa. It warmed her heart to see it and it only confirmed what she'd concluded about Riley.

She was a good person with a good heart.

She wasn't sure why she was surprised. She'd suspected as much when they'd first collided at the grocery store. But now, witnessing it firsthand, it resonated deeper inside her and left her almost as warm as the fire.

Zoe continued to watch while finishing her drink. Phoenix talked her into making one more, which was four total for him, and they did so together, laughing once again as they stacked the marshmallows and chocolate between the graham crackers. Phoenix once again was left covered in chocolate, and this time Elise came and scooped him up, declaring bath time.

Phoenix protested loudly and insisted on giving Zoe a hug.

"Are you gonna be here in the morning?" he said, throwing himself against her.

"Phoenix," Keira said from the couch. "Come on, hon, it's time to go."

He protested some more, but Elise managed to get him to follow her and the three of them disappeared into the kitchen, headed for the hallway, leaving her and Riley all alone.

"He's really something special," Zoe said, looking after them.

"He is."

Zoe looked back at the fire. She could feel Riley's eyes on her.

"I get the feeling you are too," she said.

Zoe looked at her. Locked into those blazing irises. She blushed fiercely and fought for something to say. Her heart careened and her bones melted and she wanted more than anything to just sit there and look into her eyes forever. But instead she panicked.

"I should probably get going."

"Wait," Riley said, reaching out to touch her face. Her fingertips were so soft, so gentle, Zoe almost wondered if they were real. "You've got some chocolate," she thumbed her cheek, "right here." She rubbed it off and held her gaze for a long moment. Zoe swore that if she'd closed her eyes right then, that Riley would've leaned in and kissed her.

And what surprised her the most was how the very thought of that excited her to no end.

CHAPTER NINE

Zoe stood and Riley quickly rose alongside her. "I'm sorry, I didn't mean to—"

"No, it's okay. I really should be getting back. I have a long walk ahead of me."

Riley followed her to the coat rack where they both slid into their coats. Riley dug in her pockets and retrieved her gloves. She eyed Zoe's bare hands and gave them to her. "Here. Take them, please. And..." She hurried through the kitchen into the front of the house, dug through some bags of winter clothes she'd yet to unpack, and brought one out for Zoe.

Zoe appeared surprised as she handed it over.

"For you. Clothes. And some blankets."

"Riley, I—"

"Please take it. It's the least I can do."

Zoe hesitated but then took the bag. She hoisted it up over her shoulder and opened the door looking a little like Santa with his bounty of gifts. Riley followed her out and closed the door behind them. She led the way down the patio steps to her old Bronco. She unlocked the passenger side first.

"Wait, are you—coming with me?" Zoe asked.

"I'm driving you, yes."

"But—"

"This I am insisting on. I'm not about to let you walk all the way back up this mountain alone in the freezing darkness. I feel bad enough letting you go in the first place, but I know you'll decline staying here, so I didn't bother asking."

Riley stopped in front of the vehicle and stared at her. "I'm right about that, aren't I? You are welcome to stay here, you know. You can sleep on the couch."

"Your friends," Zoe said, "are uncomfortable I can tell."

"It's my cabin. And you're a human being. A very nice human being as far as I can tell, so to me it's not right that you're sleeping out in this freezing weather. I mean, my God, it's supposed to snow soon."

"I—appreciate the offer but I can't."

"Why?"

She shook her head. "It doesn't matter. I just can't."

Riley sighed and climbed in the driver's door. Zoe did the same on the passenger side and they started up the trail, headlights lighting up cones of visibility in front of them.

Riley cranked the heat, which by some miracle still worked, and drove slowly, hoping to keep her warm for as long as possible.

"Does the SUV belong to Keira and Elise?" Zoe asked.

"No, it's mine. I just keep this old girl up here to drive around on the trails. It's fun, and truthfully, I just can't seem to let her go."

"I understand," she said. "I love old cars."

Riley watched her for a few seconds, thinking about continuing the conversation about cars, but then changing her mind. Her curiosity getting the better of her.

"I wish you would tell me what's going on with you," Riley said. "I'm not going to hurt you. I hope you know that."

"I know that, Riley. And I appreciate all that you've done. Really I do. I just—it has nothing to do with you or my trust in you. It's just—complicated." She hung her head to stare at her hands.

"Can you at least tell me if you are safe? I get the sense you're not."

She sat quietly.

"Zoe?"

"I'll be fine," she finally said.

Okaay.

Riley sighed again. "You know I'm not going to sleep tonight knowing you are out here all alone. It scares me just to think about it."

Zoe looked at her. "I'm all right. Really. It's very quiet and nobody bothers me."

"How long are you planning on being here, on doing this?"

She shrugged. "I don't know yet."

"Are you homeless? Do you have a place to live somewhere?" She didn't seem to be homeless to Riley. Her clothes seemed newer and so did her supplies.

"I have a home," she said softly.

"Then why aren't you there?"

Zoe was quiet for a long moment. "I needed to get away. Just for a while. Haven't you ever needed to get away?"

Riley hesitated. "Sure, I guess."

"It's why you have your cabin, isn't it?"

"I suppose so."

"Well, then you understand."

"Yes, but you have no place to go to. You have a tent. And it's winter."

"I have a place," she said, almost so softly Riley couldn't hear her.

"You do?"

She nodded. "My grandfather's."

"But I thought—"

"His cabin is still standing. I'm staying there as of today."

Riley released a long breath. "Oh, thank God." She smiled at her. "That makes me feel so much better."

Zoe returned the smile. "Good, I'm glad."

"So do you have everything you need? Food etc.? We can go back and get some food. Damn it, I should've thought of food."

"I'm fine, Riley."

"You can't be living off those granola bars. You know that, right?"

"You know I have granola bars?"

"The grocery store. We bumped into one another, remember?"

"Right."

"Tell me you have more than granola bars."

"I—can't."

"Oh, my God. We're turning around."

"Riley, no." She reached out and held tight to the wheel. "Please, just take me home."

"But you—"

"If you want to bring me food you can do it tomorrow. Okay?"

Riley nodded. Zoe released the steering wheel.

"But you have to promise me one thing," Zoe said.

"You got it."

"You cannot, under any circumstance, tell anyone I'm here. You haven't seen me, haven't ever met me. Okay?"

Riley blinked, confused. "Why?"

"Just promise me."

Riley swallowed, her mind racing over the possibilities as to why she needed to keep her presence a secret. None of them were good.

"Okay," she whispered.

"I know that probably scares you and I'm sorry about that. But really, Riley, it should. For your own protection. Actually, you should probably just stay away from me."

"Have you—done something?"

Zoe looked down at her hands once again. "No. I've done nothing wrong."

"Then I don't understand."

"I don't expect you to."

She looked up and pointed. "You're going to turn just past here."

Riley slowed the Bronco and made the turn.

"You can stop here. I'll walk the rest of the way."

Riley shook her head. "No, I'll take you the whole way."

"You can't."

"Why not?"

"Because, okay? Stop the car."

Riley stopped and watched helplessly as she climbed out. She gave her a quick wave and headed off into the beams of light. Riley stayed parked until she disappeared into the darkness. Then she turned around and headed for home.

Wondering all the while why Zoe didn't want her to see hers.

Chapter Ten

S he's a criminal," Elise said as she sipped her second cup of hot cocoa.

Riley rubbed her forehead and then sipped from her own mug. The butterscotch schnapps really added some great flavor. But it was lost on her at the moment. Phoenix was in bed and she and Keira and Elise were up talking and drinking, waiting for the fire to die down. Riley had just filled them in on her trek with Zoe.

"No, I don't get the sense that she is."

"Forgive me, Riley, but I'm not interested in your senses," Elise said.

Keira nudged her. "What she means to say is that it is very concerning that this woman, this stranger, seems to be hiding away up here, wanting no one to know she's here. You get that, right, Riley?"

"Of course I get that. But I'm telling you, I don't think she's a criminal or anything remotely close to that. I just don't get that from her."

Elise scoffed. "Riley, do you remember when we were kids and you brought home every stray animal that you found? Well, this isn't like that. She's not a lost little puppy. You can't bring her home and save her."

"I know that, Elise. But she is human."

"And she's not your responsibility."

"I'm not saying she is."

"No, but you want to save her."

"I want to *help* her. My God, Elise, it's freezing out there. She was in a tent. A tent." She sighed and rubbed her forehead again. "Remember when we were kids and you had a heart?"

Keira laughed and Elise gave a "very funny" smirk.

"Seriously, you're like the Grinch now. Your heart seems to be two sizes too small."

Keira laughed harder and Elise pinched her thigh causing her to gasp. "Keep laughing and this Grinch will ice you out in bed tonight."

Keira closed her mouth but struggled to stifle her laugh. She hugged her from behind and pulled her in close, wrapping her legs around her.

"You're such a hard-ass," she said, kissing her ear. "Nobody knows how kind and passionate you really are. Nobody but me."

"And maybe you're one too many," she retorted.

"Can we get back to Zoe please?"

"What about her, Ri? If you want to help her, then help her," Keira said. "I don't agree with it, but then again we're leaving tomorrow night so I won't be around to object. Just promise us you'll be careful."

Riley set down her mug and stared into the dying fire.

"I will. I'll help her. And I'll be careful."

And I'll do it first thing tomorrow after you guys leave.

CHAPTER ELEVEN

He inhaled on his unlit cigarette as he looked over at the dog in the passenger seat. She was small and white, some sort of terrier mix, with scruffy fur. She was cute enough, even if she was already a pain in the ass.

"You ought to be thanking me, dog," he said. "I just saved your life."

But the dog seemed clueless, anxiously staring out the window, standing up on her back paws, tail wagging like crazy. Her wet snout was marking up the glass.

"Hey, watch it. This isn't my car."

He reached over and tugged on her leash, pulling her away from the window. That didn't stop her attempt to get back to it though.

"All right, all right. We'll get out."

He opened his door and stepped out, allowing the little dog to follow. She hopped out eagerly and began tugging on the lead, nose to the ground. He closed the car door and locked it, noting once again how sharp the black Ford Mustang was. All black with dark tinted windows gave it a fierce, menacing look. A look he liked. It was his favorite car to take home from the dealership even if he couldn't smoke in it.

He was lucky that way. That his job allowed him to drive different vehicles whenever he wanted. It helped him with his monitoring. Different cars on the street drew less attention. And the less he was noticed, the better.

Today, however, he had to take a chance.

Enter the dog.

The mutt, whose name was Annie, according to the rescue shelter, was pulling on him, anxious to get going. He followed her in the darkness down the sidewalk toward the house. Her house. Zoe. The woman he couldn't get from his mind.

There was still no movement and hadn't been for a couple of days now. He'd called her work on Friday when she hadn't emerged for her run, and they'd told him she was out sick. They'd asked if they could take a message and he'd declined and hung up. If she was sick then everything made sense. It could be why she hadn't come out, why she hadn't run. But something just didn't feel right about it.

The lights. They went on and off at the exact same time, yesterday and today. Almost as if they were on a timer.

Her phone. Incoming calls had been ignored. And there were none outgoing and there were no answered texts.

Something was off. And it was driving him mad.

He'd done nothing but go over it and over it the last forty-eight hours. He had to know. And he had to know now.

He crossed the street and led Annie up on the adjacent sidewalk. They were three houses down from the target. His heart began to race as he drew closer. He swallowed against a dry throat as his senses awakened and intensified. He heard a distant dog bark. It was small, like Annie. A yipper, as his mother would say. He heard laughter coming from a nearby house. Smelled the smoke from someone's backyard grill. People were home and relaxing, so he'd have to be careful.

He pulled down on his ball cap and picked up his pace as they approached the house. Once there, he stopped and allowed Annie an opportunity to sniff around, giving him the opportunity to try to look inside. To his dismay, the blinds were still closed, so he couldn't see. But as they moved along the sidewalk closer to the front door, a light came on. A motion sensor light. And he saw what he needed to see.

Two folded newspapers on the front porch right by the door. He hadn't seen them earlier due to the dim light of her covered entryway. But now he was seeing.

And he knew then that something was terribly wrong.

Because she always picked up her newspapers.

That, he knew for sure.

It was time to kick things into high gear.

CHAPTER TWELVE

The snow had started falling an hour before, just as Keira, Elise, and Phoenix were leaving. Phoenix had cried, wanting to stay and play in it, and Riley had soothed him by telling him he could come back and they'd build a snowman and have a snowball fight. He made her promise and she did, even pinky swearing with him. That had calmed him, and after a long hug, Keira picked him up and put him in his booster seat.

"You going to be okay without the SUV for a while?" Elise asked. They needed to return home so Keira could work, but Riley had planned to stay. So she suggested the trio take her SUV so they'd have a way back up. Because a Prius just didn't cut it on this mountain.

"I have the Bronco. I'll be fine."

"Yeah, right. No offense, Riley, but that girl should've been put out of her misery years ago. You'll be lucky if she continues to start in this weather," Keira said.

"I'll be fine. Besides, this was the plan all along. You guys ride up with me and leave me while you return home to work. Then you bring the 4Runner back, stay another weekend, and get me. And to tell you the truth, being stranded in a cabin as the beautiful snow falls all around me sounds like heaven. Just so you know." She'd been looking forward to it for months.

"You're crazy," Elise said, hugging her. "I'd be scared to death."

"Nah. I've got plenty of supplies and like I said, I have the Bronco and don't forget the ATV. So no worries."

"You be careful with that woman now. Promise?" Elise was holding her face and the tiny flakes of snow felt like pinpricks of ice.

"Do I have to pinky swear to you, too?"

"Yes, as a matter of fact." She held out her pinky and Riley laughed.

"Get out of here."

"I mean it," Elise said, rounding the vehicle. "Be careful."

"Yes, Mother," Riley called out.

"She's worried," Keira said, enveloping her in an embrace.

"I'll be fine. You'll only be gone a couple of weeks. What can happen in two weeks?"

Keira sighed and drew away. "With you? God, there's no telling."

Riley slugged her playfully. "Go. Worrywarts. Go before it really starts coming down."

Keira glanced up at the sky. "Keep an eye on the weather," she said. "They could be wrong about the severity of this storm."

"Go!"

"Okay, okay." She climbed in the SUV, waved, and then drove away.

Now Riley was accelerating in the Bronco, trying to make it to Zoe's as quickly as she could. The sun would set soon and the snowfall was increasing.

What she failed to mention to Keira and Elise was just how worthless the Bronco and ATV would be in the heavy snow. She'd need a snowmobile if she wanted to get anywhere in a storm like this, and that was one thing she didn't have.

She slowed as she came to the turnoff that Zoe had showed her the night before. Carefully, she made her way down the trail, squinting to make out a cabin in the brush. She found it quickly, hidden in the trees, and the relief she'd felt the night before when

Zoe told her she was staying there, left her in a gasp. The cabin was tiny, maybe two rooms, and it had definitely seen better days. The exterior appeared to be worn and ramshackle, and a window had a break in it. A break big enough for cold air to seep right through. Now she understood why Zoe didn't want her to see it.

She killed the engine as Zoe emerged, hugging herself in her heavy coat.

"You found me."

"Wasn't hard."

That didn't seem to comfort her any.

Riley climbed from the Bronco and pulled out the large backpack of food she'd brought for her. As she walked up to her, she saw that Zoe was shivering, her face ashen, her lips dry and pale.

"Jesus, you're freezing." Riley dropped the bag and held her shoulders.

"I'm fine. Just a little cold."

"Do you not have any heat?" She looked past her, trying to see into the cabin. When she went to move, to step around Zoe, Zoe grew nervous.

"It's just a little run-down. I need to fix it up."

Riley pushed open the door, now hell-bent on seeing for herself.

"Don't, I—"

But Riley was already inside, mouth agape. She blinked in disbelief. The cabin was damn near about to fall down around her. Cold wind whistled through the walls and through the broken window. Snow fell in the corner where there was a hole in the roof. And the fireplace, well, there wasn't one. Just an old stove turned on its side, door missing.

On the floor, on the other side of the cabin, was Zoe's tent. She'd had to pitch the tent in her own cabin. It was a wonder she hadn't totally frozen.

"Get your stuff, we're going," Riley said. She bypassed her to put the food back in the Bronco.

"Riley, I'm fine, I—"

"Don't argue," Riley said. "You won't win."

Zoe attempted to laugh. It sounded weak. "You can't make me."

"I can, and I will." Riley walked back to her. "So, we can do this the hard way or the easy way. Either way, you're coming with me."

Zoe's eyes were wide again, and she looked like a frightened animal. "But I can't—"

"I don't want to hear it. You're coming with me."

"But—"

"Whatever the hell it is you think is going to happen can just happen. And it can happen at my place. I no longer care. Because if I let you stay here you're going to die of hypothermia. That I know for sure. So get your things, only what you really need, and get in the Bronco. We'll talk about the rest later."

Zoe stared at her for a long moment. When she finally spoke, Riley could hardly hear her.

"I'll get my clothes." She gathered them up in the sack and followed Riley back outside. She walked slowly to the Bronco and climbed in. Riley started the vehicle and turned around. Then they sped off into the approaching twilight, snow now falling harder than ever.

CHAPTER THIRTEEN

Zoe sat on the couch shivering uncontrollably. She pulled the blankets Riley had draped over her tighter.

"Here we go," Riley said, returning from the kitchen. "Some hot tea."

"Thank you." Zoe took the tea and sipped delicately. The liquid was hot, almost too hot. She blew on it while trying to hold it steady with two hands.

Riley began building a fire. Outside, the sun had set and the sky was a pale orange as snow came down in a frenzied flurry. The deck was already covered and the trees coated in fluffy white. She wondered just how cold it would be tonight and whether or not Riley had been right. Would she have frozen? She was too tired to think about it. Too tired to care. At least if she died all this would be over. The game of cat and mouse would end. He would win with her demise but lose with her now gone. He'd have nothing to chase. No purpose.

He'd find himself a new one.

The thought manifested out of nowhere, but somehow she knew it to be true. He'd just move on with a new target. A man like him would never stop. Not until he died.

His obsession was never-ending.

She sipped her tea and wondered if he knew yet. If he knew she'd snuck off and left. She hoped not. She wanted a good night's rest, and fearing that he now knew would keep her up. Because she knew how angry he'd be at being beaten. At being tricked. And he'd stop at nothing to find her. She had no doubt.

Riley rose and came to sit next to her on the couch. She looked so striking in her dark green sweater and blue jeans. So cozy in her thick gray socks and waves of black hair.

"How are you doing? Are you warming up?"

Zoe tried to laugh but failed. "Can't stop shivering."

Riley smiled. "Shivering is good. If you weren't shivering I'd be concerned. Just keep drinking that tea and sitting here by the fire. You'll warm up soon."

She rested her elbow on top of the couch and leaned her head against her fist.

"You're very lucky I came for you. You would've been in bad shape in this storm. And I wouldn't have been able to get to you."

Zoe nodded. "Thank you."

"You're welcome." She crossed her legs and studied her. "I want to ask you so many things."

Zoe looked down at her mug.

"But I won't. Not now."

Zoe took another sip, finally meeting her gaze again. Riley was watching her closely, with eyes as kind as her tone.

"I'm going to go get you a bed ready. You stay right here by the fire." She winked at her and stood and walked away, and Zoe wondered what all she would tell her when the time came. She wanted to be truthful, but the truth was crazy sounding, not to mention dangerous. She was putting Riley at great risk by being there. Could she tell her that? Would Riley finally agree with her that she needed to stay away? If so, where would she go? Back to the cabin?

Riley said she would die.

Maybe it was just as well.

Maybe that was the only real way to end this.

She closed her eyes and sipped more tea. It was cooler now and she was able to swallow more. The warm liquid felt good as it fell down her throat and warmed her insides. If only something could warm her mind.

If only.

Riley returned and stoked the fire. Then she came back to the couch.

"Your room's all set. Nice warm bed."

"Thank you."

She laughed. "No need to keep thanking me. Once was enough."

"Sorry."

"No need to apologize either." She reached out and touched her hand. "You're safe here. Just let that sink in."

Oh God, I wish that were true.

"I'll try."

Riley patted her hand. "Is there anyone you'd like to call? To let them know—"

"No!"

Riley blinked. "Okay."

"Sorry, I just—no, no thank you."

Riley appeared gravely concerned. But instead of asking her more questions, she simply brushed her fingers across Zoe's cheek.

"Hey, you are safe here. Rest easy in that."

Zoe's breath hitched as she fought tears. "Okay." She grabbed Riley's hand, clutched it in her own, too afraid to let her continue. Because if she did, Zoe wasn't sure if she'd break down in tears or throw herself in her arms. Neither one would be her best move. Not if she wanted to come across as sane.

Riley inhaled deeply and squeezed her hand. "You've stopped shivering."

Zoe laughed. She knew it was from the rush of heat Riley's touch had ignited, but she didn't share that.

"Guess it was the tea."

"I did spike it, you know."

"Yes. I can feel it."

"Good, you need to relax a little. How about a hot shower?"

Zoe closed her eyes. "I don't think anything has ever sounded so good."

Riley released her hand and tapped her leg. "Come on then. I'll show you your room and the bathroom so you can make yourself right at home."

Home.

Zoe wondered what the word would mean to her in the days to come.

CHAPTER FOURTEEN

Riley rolled over and cinched the covers tighter around her. The pale light of a stormy dawn seeped in through the curtains, and she could feel the chill in the air on her face. The duvet encased her in warmth, and she debated whether or not to climb out of bed and into the cold morning air. She was so comfortable in her bed. So snug and warm and—Zoe.

She'd nearly forgotten about her guest.

She sat up and tore off her covers. Her heart thudded as several thoughts shot through her mind at the same time. She heard Elise's voice warning her about the mysterious woman, warning her that she might be a criminal. Then her mind flew to her own worries of Zoe's safety and just what it was she was running from. And finally, her mind went the Zoe's well-being. Had she been warm enough last night? Had she recovered from the cold?

Riley shrugged into a thick robe and padded across the loft in her sock feet. She looked out the vaulted windows and saw that the snow was still coming down.

Damn. This was some storm.

She hurried down the spiral staircase and froze when she got to the bottom. There, on the couch, was Zoe sound asleep. Riley crossed to her silently, curious as to why she was on the sofa. She'd gone to bed immediately after her shower the night before.

Riley wondered when she'd gotten up and why. Was her room not warm enough?

Riley sat on the coffee table and took the time to relish in the study of her. Zoe was snoring softly, completely wiped out, arm draped above her head, waves of chestnut hair spilling down around her shoulders. One leg was protruding out from the heavy blanket, knee bent, resting against the back of the couch, her body lying a little crooked on the cushions. It seemed she'd slept wild and hard, oblivious to her position.

Riley secured the covers for her and tucked the blanket in around her shoulders. Zoe immediately grabbed the blanket, clutching it to her chest in a protective gesture. She appeared to be wary, even in her sleep.

Riley felt strongly for her then, wondering what in the world this angelic looking woman could be running from. She just didn't seem to be the type to be running from the law, or any sort of trouble for that matter.

"What's your story?" Riley asked softly, lightly caressing her brow. She brushed her hair back from her forehead, lost in her beautiful, peaceful face.

Zoe groaned and shifted, and Riley drew away, not wanting to wake her. Instead, she rose and busied herself making a fire. Some nice roaring flames would warm them both up and make the morning a little more welcoming.

When she finished, she stood there for a while, warming herself while staring out the window. The snowfall had slowed, showing off all that it had done the night before, completely covering the deck, the trees beyond, and the valley below. It was a sight to behold. Absolutely beautiful and serene. She could almost hear the eerie wind blowing through those trees, feel the heavy silence that would follow.

This was her first snow at the cabin, and she couldn't have imagined anything as majestic as this. She sighed wistfully and glanced back at Zoe asleep on the sofa.

"I'm in a winter wonderland with a beautiful, mysterious woman."

It was like a dream, a fantasy. But there were dark corners to this dream, she could sense them. And she just knew that darkness would soon creep in and conquer what remained of the dream. Question was, when? And would that darkness completely overtake the beautiful fantasy? Or would it leave enough for her to enjoy?

Based on the fear and worry Zoe exuded, she was guessing that darkness would consume it all.

Would either one of them be left when it did?

A chill swept through her and she hugged herself and headed to the kitchen to put on a pot of coffee. She stared out the kitchen window as she waited for it to brew and noticed how an icy frost was nestled in the corners of the windowpane. Just like that darkness to her dream.

She blinked the vision away and retrieved the bacon and eggs for breakfast. She got started making it, sipping her coffee as she did so once it was done. It woke her at once and she felt better and more positive about her day. She hoped, at the very least, she could enjoy a nice breakfast with Zoe before they got to the questions she had for her.

She scrambled the eggs and turned the bacon. The smells came alive and permeated the cabin. Zoe was stirring by the time she carried the plates to the table.

"Morning," Riley greeted her, setting the plates down. "Hope you're hungry. And I hope you're not vegan."

Zoe rubbed her eyes and messed with her hair as if she were trying to tame it.

"I am and I'm not," she rasped. She stood and smiled as she made her way into the kitchen and down the hall for the bathroom. She looked cute in Riley's sweatpants and long-sleeved shirt. Even if they were too big for her.

When she returned, she sat with Riley, reaching eagerly for her cup of coffee. "Mm, thank you, this is good."

"My pleasure. Juice?" She hovered over her glass with the pitcher of orange juice.

"Please."

Riley poured and then sipped from her own glass. "It's not much. Just scrambled eggs and turkey bacon."

"It's wonderful," she said. "After countless granola bars, this feels like a feast." She dug in and then seemed to realize how quickly she was eating and slowed. She touched her mouth. "Sorry. I guess I'm a little hungrier than I thought."

"No worries," Riley said. "Eat all you want, we have plenty."

Riley noticed that Zoe's color had returned, and her prominent cheek bones were brushed with it, like an artist had deftly run a brush of crimson along the tops. She was mesmerizing in the morning light, her whiskey irises reflective and seeking, the highlights of her hair nearly matching the color as it fell in wild layers upon her shoulders. Riley had to force herself to look away and concentrate on her meal.

"How did you sleep?" she asked.

Zoe swallowed. "Uh, not so good at first. Couldn't get settled."

"Is the bed uncomfortable?"

"No, not at all. It's—me. I felt better sleeping by the door."

Riley chuckled. "Just in case you needed to make a quick escape?"

"No," she said quietly. "To make sure nobody came in."

Riley swallowed, alarmed. She didn't like the look on her face or the words she'd spoken.

"I'm, uh, a little uncomfortable that the door doesn't close so well."

"It's old, but it does lock. So, you have nothing to worry about."

Zoe nodded.

Riley cleared her throat. "We'll talk about all that after breakfast. For now, let's enjoy our meal."

Zoe nodded slowly and picked at her food. She seemed to have lost her appetite.

"Please, eat," Riley said softly. "I know you're hungry."

"I think my stomach shrank. I'm already full." She sipped her juice and then went back to her coffee. She avoided Riley's gaze and Riley knew the moment had been lost.

It seemed those dark corners were already beginning to creep in.

CHAPTER FIFTEEN

He studied his computer and clenched his jaw. He went over his list next to the keyboard noting all the checked off names. He had a few more to investigate, two of them out of town. How was he going to do that? He couldn't just take off and head for Texas. He'd lose his job for sure.

He took his pen and hovered above the list. He'd already checked out her immediate family and close friends. He'd already had a feel for their daily habits just by watching her when she visited them. There were only five of them, and he was reasonably certain she wasn't there. How did he know? Because they were blowing up her phone, leaving voice mails, some of them becoming frantic, pleading for her to return their calls.

Next, he assumed, would be a wellness check. One of her loved ones would go to her house, knock on the door, and get no answer. Then they'd call the police to check on her. It could, for all he knew, even be happening right now while he was stuck at work.

God, he hated his job. The only good thing about it was the personal information he could get on people when they financed a vehicle. That and all the cars he got to choose from to drive home every night. The manager loved him and allowed him to just about have his pick of the lot. His favorite though, was the all-black Mustang. That beat the hell out of his Fusion sitting in his garage. The Mustang was mean, fierce, a force to be reckoned with. Just like who he really was on the inside. It was both fortunate and unfortunate that everybody else only saw the Fusion side of him. The safe, polite, wallflower that every mother in Phoenix wanted to set her daughter up with.

God, he hated it. He wanted to choose his own woman, not be set up with some older single woman who, for whatever reason, couldn't get a man. No way. And frankly, it insulted him.

Now he'd found the one who had been eluding him. Finally. After all these years. Life was funny that way. You never knew who was going to walk through your door.

This one, Zoe. She was the one, he knew it without a doubt. Knew it the second she'd walked in his office and pinned those copper-like irises on him. Holy shit. He'd about fallen out of his chair. She had no clue. Figured. Story of his life. And that was going to be the tough part. He had to get to her now to get her to turn around and see things his way. See that they belonged together and that she belonged to him. He just had to get her first. Take her somewhere safe, like his home, where he could keep her and work on convincing her. And if that didn't work, well, he had a plan B. Zoe would do good to see things his way. She would not like plan B. But he would do whatever he had to to keep her. She was not going to get away. No way. No how.

So what if she got a jump on him. She was clever. And feisty. He liked that. And really it had been his own fault. He'd waited too long and teased her, toying with her, like a mischievous cat with a frightened mouse. He should've made his move sooner and taken her.

But now here he was, doing his best to sift through her loved ones, to find the one she ran to, if she ran to one. Based on what he knew so far, he was thinking she'd gone somewhere on her own. Again, clever. And courageous. God, how he wanted her.

And whether she knew it or not, this little game she'd put into play was only turning him on all the more. He loved a good chase, a good mystery. Even if it did aggravate him and make him spend hours on end trying to find the solution. It was all part of the game.

A game he loved to play.

CHAPTER SIXTEEN

"Ican wash your clothes if you like," Riley said as Zoe made her way back into the living room.

"Oh. Okay." She hesitated before she sat. "I can do it if you show me where everything is."

"It's no trouble. But I'll show you where everything is so you can do it yourself if you're more comfortable." She smiled and patted the couch, pulling her own legs up to tuck beneath her.

Zoe sat and smoothed her hands over the thick, soft sweats. She was finally warm, and she couldn't believe it. It was like her body had grown accustomed to shivering. She expected it to start up at any moment, despite being warm, as if the shivering had a mind of its own.

"You look well," Riley said. "Rested." She sipped from her mug of coffee. Zoe noticed that she'd made one for her as well. It sat steaming on the coffee table. She grabbed it and took a small sip. It was delicious. She eased back on the couch and tried to relax, though she knew what was coming next and she wasn't looking forward to it. She'd actually debated just up and leaving and heading back to the cabin to take her chances rather than deal with what was to come.

But Riley had been so nice. She at least owed her some sort of an explanation. Even if it meant losing her support.

"I was worried about you, you know," Riley said. "You looked so pale and weak. Wasn't sure you'd be okay, even after getting you here."

"I'm okay," she said. "Thanks to you."

She shifted her gaze to look into the fire. The way Riley was looking at her was warming her up in a whole new way.

"You look good in my clothes."

Zoe pulled in a deep breath and hoped Riley didn't notice. She kept her own eyes on the fire, unsure what to say. Was Riley flirting with her, or was it just an innocent observation?

Either way, Zoe knew she needed to confide in her, and if Riley was flirting, telling her the truth would surely put a stop to that. Zoe needed to put a stop to that before Riley grew too fond of her.

"So you wanted to talk?" Zoe finally turned to face her, and she saw Riley blink in apparent surprise. She set her mug on the coffee table and cleared her throat. Zoe's heart nearly stampeded in her chest at the anticipation.

"I was hoping you would tell me what's going on with you. What it is you're running from, or hiding from."

Zoe held her gaze for a moment before lowering it to the couch. She couldn't bear to look at her for fear that she'd see everything inside her. All the fear, the shame, the anguish. That she'd see how truly weak she was.

"I—I—" She sighed and rubbed her forehead.

"It's okay. Take your time."

Zoe shook her head, trying to shake away the hesitation. "I don't know who I'm running from." She looked up at her and saw the confusion on her face. "I mean—I'm not sure who he is. I just know that he watches me. That he—"

"You have a stalker?"

Zoe swallowed. "Yes."

Riley seemed to think for a moment. "But you don't know who he is?"

"No. I mean I think I've seen him a couple of times. But I can't make out his face and I don't know—I just know I'm being watched."

"Why? What's happened?"

Zoe sighed again. "My email has been hacked into, along with my personal accounts, everything. It took me a while to figure it out, and once I did and I changed passwords and even got new accounts, he started messing with me. Messing with those things. Nothing like stealing or anything. Just little things. Things only I would notice. And then he started leaving me things. Like flowers, on my car windshield."

"Have you gone to the police?"

Zoe nodded. "They told me I don't have any evidence of anything illegal being done. So they told me to keep a record of all that's happening and to come back when I had something more, like if he threatened me for instance."

"And he hasn't? Threatened you that is?"

"Not in so many words. But his constant subtle harassment is threat enough for me."

"What else has he done?"

"He messes with my incoming and outgoing email and postal mail. I get mysterious phone calls from unavailable numbers where someone is just sitting there on the other end of the line. Sometimes he leaves me flowers, and sometimes, when I'm running or working out, he leaves me a towel and a water bottle."

"What?"

"Yeah. If I'm at the gym, he leaves it on my car."

"Oh my God, he follows you too?"

"Yes."

"Jesus, that's scary."

Zoe looked down into her coffee. "You have no idea."

"I can't imagine. I'm so sorry, Zoe."

Zoe shrugged. "It is what it is."

"How long has this been going on?"

"About a year. Probably longer and I just didn't realize."

"Have you told anybody else, other than the police?"

"My family and friends know. Some believe me, others think I'm being ridiculous. They just tell me I have a secret admirer."

"A secret admirer that hacks into your personal accounts? I don't think so."

"The ones who do believe me just keep telling me to go to the police. But I've done that and even they looked at me like I was nuts."

"Nice. Aren't there laws about hacking and things like that?"

"Sure, if I can prove it. But I don't have the know-how and I don't have a lot of extra money to hire somebody who does."

"Yeah, I can see how you're stuck." She seemed to think for a moment. "So what happened to make you up and leave and come up here with little in the way of supplies?"

Zoe swallowed. "He, uh—he scared me. Really scared me."

"How so?"

"I was talking to my aunt on the phone, about him, about what's been going on, and suddenly, there was this laughter. This god-awful laughter over the line. It sounded so sinister. So evil. It wasn't my aunt and she couldn't hear it."

The color seemed to drain from Riley's face. "He's somehow messing with your phone, too."

"Yes."

"Oh my God. That is scary. Really scary."

"It made me feel like he was closer than I knew. Like maybe he was even in my house. I searched my home up and down and didn't sleep. Couldn't sleep. I did nothing but think about a way to escape. A place to run to. That's when I saw the photo on my mantle of my grandfather and me at this cabin. And suddenly I knew what to do. I purchased timers for my lights, told work I wasn't feeling well and wouldn't be in the next day, and set off up here with what gear I had. I figured I'd only stay a few days. Maybe just enough time to reset and figure out what to do next."

"I understand."

"I just want peace. I just want the same freedoms everyone else has."

"Sure, I get it and I don't blame you. But how do you know he won't find you here?"

"I don't, really. But it was the best place I knew of. It's off-grid and no one in my family has been up here in years. My grandfather's passed. I didn't bring my phone with me, or anything like that. And I didn't tell anyone I was leaving. I couldn't risk that. Especially since he seems to be messing with my phone."

"Did he not see you leave?"

"I guess not. I left at two a.m. and drove up. I left my car and got a ride up to the mountain here. So, odds are, I'll have at least a few days' peace."

"What do you think he'll do when he knows you're gone?"

"I don't know."

"But you're worried."

Zoe met her gaze. "Yes. I'm afraid it will really piss him off."

"I'd be concerned too."

Zoe laughed. "I didn't know it was going to snow like this. I didn't even think about a snowstorm. I don't know what I was thinking."

"Sounds like you've had a lot of other things on your mind. Understandably so."

Riley grew quiet for a moment. "Zoe?"

"Yes?"

"What were you going to do if I hadn't come for you?"

She shrugged. "I don't know."

"Would you have tried to leave?"

"I don't know."

"You know it was very dangerous to be out here like that, right?"

Zoe looked at her. "Honestly, Riley, I just didn't even care at that point."

Riley pressed her lips together and nodded.

She didn't say another word.

CHAPTER SEVENTEEN

Riley wasn't sure what was worse. Knowing or not knowing. There was a little relief with learning that she'd been right and Zoe wasn't a criminal of some sort. That is, if she was telling the truth. But Riley didn't sense she was lying. She seemed too scared, even to get the words out. She'd even trembled a few times while discussing it.

There was also the possibility that Zoe was overreacting and maybe being a bit paranoid. But even if she was, the obvious truth was that she was scared. Scared to death. Scared enough to hike up a mountain with little provisions and camp out in the middle of a snowstorm with no intention of leaving for safer ground. If she was willing to do that, then Riley had to assume that at the very least Zoe believed what she was saying. And that was enough for her to believe as well.

"I know you're frightened," Riley said, watching as Zoe hugged herself from across the sofa. "But I really do think you're safe here. If your family no longer comes up here and you didn't bring anything he can trace you with, then you should be fine."

"I hope you're right. I want you to be right. But you don't understand how thorough this person seems to be. It's like they'll stop at nothing."

"That's another thing I wanted to ask you," Riley said. "How do you know it's a man?"

"I guess I don't really know for sure. Although I do think I've seen him a few times. He's always in the shadows and always wearing a ball cap. But I can't be sure it's the same person or necessarily that it's a man. But why would a woman do this to me?"

"You'd be surprised. Women get obsessed too. You haven't recently pissed anyone off have you? Stolen someone's man?" Riley laughed a little, but Zoe didn't join her.

"No—I—don't—" She let the sentence drop and cleared her throat.

They were both silent for a moment. Then Riley spoke again. "Is it possible you dated someone who didn't like taking no for an answer?"

"I haven't dated for quite some time and my last relationship ended amicably. He was just as relieved to end things as I was."

Riley finished her coffee and set her mug down. "Well, hopefully you'll be able to rest easy here for the time being. Even if this person did manage to follow you up here, they'd have a heck of a time finding you in this storm. The trail up can be pretty tight and treacherous, with or without snow."

"I suppose you're right."

"I'd say I probably am." She smiled at her. "Just ask Keira, she'll tell you I am almost always right."

Zoe seemed to try for a smile in return, but it fell short. "I really appreciate you letting me stay here. You have no idea what it means to me. Especially now, knowing that you could be in danger too."

Riley nodded, understanding her fear. "Let's not think about that, okay? You're in a nice cabin in the middle of a beautiful snowstorm, so you can relax, kick your feet up for a while."

Zoe rubbed her hands on her pants as if she were nervous. "I suppose."

"You're not going to relax are you?"

"I'll try."

Riley leaned forward and held her hand. "That's all you can do." She released her and leaned back. "You know I have the same problem."

"Pardon?"

"Relaxing. My friends tell me I'm impossible when it comes to taking it easy."

"Even with this cabin?"

Riley glanced around, taking in the marvel she'd recently purchased. "I haven't had it very long. And yes, I still have trouble sitting back and kicking my feet up. I'd rather be working on this place or cutting firewood or going for a hike in the back woods. Anything but sitting still."

"But it's snowing out. So, what are you going to do now?"

"I don't know. I guess I'll have to find things to do. Or, God help me, I might actually have to relax."

Zoe laughed.

"It's nice to see you smile," Riley said. She had a gorgeous smile with a cute dimple in her left cheek. "Maybe we can help each other relax, what do you say?"

Zoe shrugged. "Sure. It's worth a shot."

"So, what do we do first?"

Zoe searched the cabin from her position on the couch. "Got any good books?"

"Tons."

"Want to read?"

"Not one little bit. You?"

"I don't think I could settle down and concentrate."

They sat in silence for a moment before Riley spoke again. "Wanna make s'mores?"

Zoe held her stomach. "I'm still full from breakfast."

"Hot chocolate and schnapps?"

"That I could go for."

Riley hopped up, happy to have something else to do other than sitting and staring at Zoe whose beauty was getting to her in more ways than one. "I'll get on it."

Chapter Eighteen

R eady?" Zoe asked as Riley positioned the handle on the cabinet door.

"Ready."

Zoe inserted the screws and screwed them tightly into to place. When she finished, Riley tugged a few times to make sure the new handle was secure.

"That's it. Great job." She rested her hands on her thighs from her position on her knees where they'd settled to work on the lower cabinets. "We're all finished."

Zoe looked up at the new pewter handles now adorning the cabinets and drawers. They looked so much better than the dated brass ones that had been on there before.

Riley stood and held her hand out for Zoe. Zoe took it and allowed Riley to pull her to a stand. Her right leg was asleep and she stumbled a bit, falling into Riley who caught her quickly.

"Whoa, you okay?"

Zoe struggled for breath as she leaned against her chest. She drew away slowly, too afraid to hold her gaze, too afraid to glance away. "Yes, sorry. My leg fell asleep."

Riley held her arms, steadying her. "Can you walk?"

Zoe nodded and Riley released her. Zoe limped into the living room. "What's next?" They'd spent the better part of the last few days doing odd jobs around the house, trying to stay busy, trying their best to distract themselves from the fact that they were trapped together all alone in a cabin during a snowstorm.

Zoe couldn't help but wonder if she made Riley's heart beat faster like she did hers. Or if she thought about what it would be like to kiss her by the fire. Or hold her tight under the blankets on the couch. Or touch her face, her skin, her lips—

"I don't know. I thought about hanging some curtains up in my bedroom."

Zoe coughed and settled on the couch. Riley was still coming up with things to do. And now she wanted to go up to her bedroom.

Could it really be that she was feeling the same way, wanting continued distractions? Or was she really just a busybody like she'd said earlier?

It didn't matter. Because either way, Riley was waiting at the bottom of the spiral staircase.

"What do you say? You up for it?"

Zoe fought for her voice. "Okay."

Riley smiled that broad, beautiful smile of hers and motioned with her hand for Zoe to go first.

"Just in case you lose your balance," Riley said with a wink.

Zoe shook out her leg and headed up the stairs, moving slowly, blushing fiercely, knowing Riley was inches behind her with an ample view of her backside.

When she finally made it to the top, her nerves didn't settle any. They actually intensified as she took in the distressed, solid pinewood bed against the left wall, covered with a dark red velvet duvet and big, fluffy looking pillows. The low evening light was coming through the curtains already hanging, giving the room a soft golden glow. Zoe took a few steps in and inhaled a scent that sent shockwaves through her body. It was the scent Riley wore; she knew it at once. It smelled of white rose and green apple with a hint of blond woods and cedar. It made her blush burn hotter. She covered her cheeks, fearing Riley would see.

"What do you think?" Riley asked. "You like it?" She walked past her and headed for the closet.

"Hm?"

"My room. Do you like what I've done to it so far?" The furniture had the same distressed driftwood appearance as the bed with notable accent pieces that played off the color of the duvet. The artwork was tasteful and abstract, giving the room a modern feel. For someone who didn't find relaxing easy, her bedroom seemed to be a haven for it. What was more relaxing than a big bed with a dark red velvet duvet in a cabin in the middle of the woods?

"Yes. It's very—" *Sensual, alluring, romantic.* "Nice."

"Nice, huh?" She chuckled and opened the closet door. "I guess I'll take that."

She pulled out the packages of new curtains. "What do you think of these?" She began to unzip the packaging and display the curtains on the bed. They were dark red striped with a tan that would bring out the color of the headboard and furniture.

"They're..."

"Nice?"

"Uh-huh."

She laughed again. "Okay. I'll take your word for it."

Zoe tried to snap to attention. "They'll look much better than what's up there."

Riley seemed pleased as she retrieved a stepladder from the closet. She set it up and climbed to remove the current curtain rod and curtains. Zoe went to her side and took them, allowing Riley to step down from the ladder. They then busied themselves threading the new curtains onto the rod. Riley climbed back up and secured the rod on her side. Then she climbed down and moved the ladder over for Zoe to do the same to her side. With Riley now holding the rod, Zoe climbed up. She took the rod from Riley and secured it on the hook. Then, as she looked down to descend, the ground seemed to move and she felt sick. She lost her balance and fell backward.

"Zoe!"

Riley caught her just in time, holding her firmly in her arms. She led her quickly over to the bed where she eased her down. Zoe clung to her, too frightened by the spinning room to let her go.

"Are you okay?" Riley asked, gently cupping her face.

Zoe tried to focus and saw those brilliant green irises.

"I got dizzy, felt sick."

Riley pressed her lips together. "You didn't eat lunch, remember? And you didn't have very much at breakfast either."

"Yeah." That was it, that had to be it. It wasn't because she was in the very seductive bedroom of this gorgeous woman she was having powerful feelings for. No, that wasn't it. Couldn't be.

Could it?

CHAPTER NINETEEN

Here," Riley said, easing her back onto the pillows. "You stay here while I go make you something to eat."

Zoe tried to sit up but failed miserably. Her head was on a ship in a very stormy sea. "Oh God." She grabbed her forehead.

"Stay." Riley left her and returned a few minutes later with a sandwich and a bottle of Snapple Iced Tea.

"This should help," Riley said as she set the tray down on the night table. She handed over the plate with the sandwich. "It's turkey on rye. Hope that's okay."

Zoe nodded. "Thanks." She took a small bite, tasted the mustard, and immediately felt better. Her hunger kicked in and she continued to eat, sipping the peach flavored iced tea as she did so.

"Good?"

"Mm-hm."

Riley smiled. She brushed Zoe's hair back from her face. "Guess I gotta keep a better eye on you."

Zoe touched her lips as she swallowed. "I think it's because I haven't been eating very much the past few days and it happened to catch up to me today."

"That and all the stress you've been under," Riley said, skimming her cheek with her fingertips.

Zoe felt herself blush and Riley pulled away and shifted on the bed.

What just happened? Had Riley seen her blush? Had she felt the heat her touch had elicited? Embarrassment coursed through her and made the sick feeling return. She had to put down the sandwich.

"I'm sorry if I disturbed you," Riley said, glancing toward the window.

"You didn't."

"I think I may have."

Zoe watched her in silence.

"I'm in quite a spot here," Riley said.

"What do you mean?"

She looked at her and smiled softly. "Nothing. Forget I said anything."

"Have I done something wrong?" She couldn't help but notice the look of regret clouding her face. Was she the cause?

"No, no of course not. It's…me. I—well, you know I'm gay, right?"

"Yes. I mean I assumed after what Phoenix said about you not having a girlfriend." *And, well, because you're gorgeous in a beautiful tomboyish kind of way. And because the way you look at me sometimes, like just now, leaves me breathless.*

"Well, I—I don't know." She exhaled. "It's been a while for me. Since I've had someone. Maybe too long."

Zoe swallowed as she began to understand what she was trying to say. Was this really happening? Was Riley about to tell her she was attracted to her? The anticipation was like torture as she sat and waited. Riley just continued to stare out the window.

Then she stood. "I better get out there and shovel the patio and the side path while there's a break in the storm." She headed for the stairs. "Please finish eating and feel free to relax up here if you like. I'll be back in a few."

"Don't you want some help?"

Riley chuckled. "You need some serious R&R for a bit, don't you think? Besides, I only have the one shovel." She winked at her. "Just relax, okay? And eat. Please." She gave her one last smile and descended the stairs.

Zoe sat staring at her sandwich and admiring the new curtains they'd just hung. Riley had good taste and she wondered what else Riley had in store for the cabin. It seemed she was doing all the work herself, which was impressive and ambitious. Now that she was getting to know Riley better, those things didn't necessarily surprise her. If anything, they left her mind reeling and wanting to know more.

She heard Riley as she began shoveling out on the deck. She was working so hard. The least Zoe could do was eat so she could recover and go and help her. She ate her sandwich slowly and sipped her tea, all the while listening to Riley's shovel scrape the patio. Snow started falling again and she found herself being lulled to sleep by the dancing snowflakes and the scrape of the shovel. Soon she was drifting off to sleep.

Zoe awoke to darkness. She lay very still, listening, but all she could hear was the beating of her own heart. She blinked as her eyes adjusted with the help of a small light in the far corner. She was in Riley's room, in her bed. Under the covers. She looked to her right and saw Riley asleep on her back. Zoe sat up, confused. The sandwich plate and iced tea bottle were gone. She pulled back the covers and discovered she was still dressed in the soft pants and long-sleeved tee Riley had given her earlier. She must've fallen asleep after she'd eaten. But how long ago was that?

"Mm, you okay?" Riley asked as she awoke.

"What happened?" She still was having trouble getting her bearings.

"I came back in from shoveling and found you sound asleep. I didn't have the heart to wake you."

Zoe looked over at her and found her in her pajamas, black hair strewn across the white pillow. God, she was gorgeous. The sight of her and the sound of her raspy voice made her heart rate triple. Not to mention the fact that they were in the same bed together.

"You were really beat," Riley said. "So I let you sleep."

Zoe closed her eyes.

"I hope that's okay," Riley said.

Zoe slowly nodded.

After a few quiet moments, she felt a soft hand on her shoulder.

"Come back to sleep."

Zoe looked back at her but hesitated. Riley seemed to sense it.

"Do you want me to go sleep downstairs?" Riley asked.

"No, this is your bed."

"It doesn't matter. You're comfortable here."

"No," Zoe said. "Don't go."

"Okay then. Come back to bed." She gently squeezed her shoulder, encouraging her to recline. Zoe did and she felt Riley shift to her side. She couldn't bear to look at her, knowing the sight of her would cause her heart to beat right out of her chest.

"Just close your eyes and go back to sleep. Everything is fine."

Zoe swallowed against a dry throat and closed her eyes. And for the first time in as many months, she actually felt like everything was indeed just fine.

CHAPTER TWENTY

She wasn't at work, and the newspapers were piling up outside her front door. Her cell phone was dead and her mailbox on the street nearing full.

Recognizance on her local friends and family proved fruitless. She wasn't there. If she was, they were hiding her awfully well.

But the phone call he'd made to her place of employment led him to believe otherwise. He'd pretended to be a family member, someone very concerned for her well-being. The woman who'd answered bought it and told him how worried they were for her, that she'd last said she was sick, and how a few other loved ones had called in as well looking for her. Including a couple from Texas. So that told him that her friends and family really didn't know where she was. They were as lost and confused as he was.

"Shh, stay," he whispered. The dog whined a little and then promptly sat in the dead grass in the backyard. He kept his palm up, encouraging her not to move as he crept along the side of the house to the back door. The lights had gone off at ten thirty and the interior of the house was dark. The neighborhood was quiet save for the sound of a distant barking dog. He entered her patio and rubbed his hands together to warm them up before slipping on his leather gloves. Then, giving Annie the dog one last glance, he approached the back French door and broke the glass with the window breaker he'd retrieved from his pocket. He had it for emergency use in his vehicle, but the thing happened to come in handy when he needed entry into a home.

He stood very still as the sound of shattering glass faded. The distant dog barked and Annie trotted up onto the patio.

"No, stay." He waved her back, not wanting her to step on the glass. She complied, whining and licking her jowls. Then he faced the door and crunched the glass beneath his work boots as he reached inside and unlocked the door. More glass broke beneath him as he stepped inside. He tugged down on his ball cap as he entered, creeping his way into the kitchen. He stopped and listened again, but there was no sound, no movement.

Just as he'd thought. She wasn't there.

He switched on his small flashlight and began searching the kitchen. He opened drawers and rifled through old calendars. Nothing. He found an address book and pocketed it. Then he moved on into the living room. The house was rather tidy so he searched the room quickly, scanning the photos on the mantle with his flashlight. He recognized some of the people in them as her loved ones, but there was one in particular he didn't recognize. It was a five-by-seven photo of her as a little girl with a man who appeared to be in his late sixties. He took the photo and slid it into the back of his waistband. He didn't have any photos of her as a little girl, so he wanted this one.

He searched through her trinkets and moved on down the hallway to her bedroom. He immediately got an erection as he caught the scent of her perfume. He crossed to the bed and sat, unscrewed a bottle of water, and sipped from it. His heart raced knowing he was drinking the very water she had. That his lips were touching the very bottle hers had. He stroked the bulge in his pants and then refocused, knowing there was no time for that. Instead he opened her nightstand and went through her belongings. And then Annie barked.

He straightened, ears perked. He closed the drawer and hurried from the bedroom and back through the living room and the kitchen. He stood at the back door and saw Annie across the moonlit lawn barking at the fence. He ran outside and whispered loudly at her. She fell silent and came to his side, tail wagging.

"Bad dog," he said through clenched teeth. He picked up her leash and led her back through the gate, peeking around the corner of the house to make sure it was clear. Then he walked her to the sidewalk and headed down the street to the car. To anyone else, he looked like a man out walking his dog in the moonlight. His cute little white dog with the bounce in her step.

His cute little white dog that had just ruined everything.

He yanked on her leash as he neared the car and cursed her as she hopped inside. He climbed in and winced as he sat, the photo in his waistband digging into his back. He closed the door and retrieved the photo, smoothing his thumbs over it in the dim dome light of the car.

She was a beautiful child and her smile lit up the photo. And she was hugging the man next to her fiercely.

"Who are you?" he asked, staring at the man. He flipped the photo over and loosened the back to remove it. He plucked the photo away from the glass and studied the handwriting on the back.

Grandpa and me. Spruce Mountain. 1994.

He smiled as he turned the photo back over and examined the cabin in the background.

Maybe Annie hadn't ruined things after all.

CHAPTER TWENTY-ONE

Has it stopped snowing?" Zoe asked as she came up to stand next to Riley at the back window.

"For now." Riley stared out at the vast white valley, watching as the wind blew flakes of snow from the trees. "Weather says more is on the way tomorrow."

Riley felt Zoe touch her arm and she turned to find her smiling softly, offering a steaming mug of what appeared to be hot chocolate.

"Thank you," Riley said, surprised. "Just what the doctor ordered."

"I hope you don't mind. I sort of helped myself in the kitchen."

"I don't mind at all. I want you to make yourself at home here."

They sat on the sofa, leaving the white wonderland as a backdrop behind them. Riley brought the mug to her lips and inhaled. It smelled a little different from the hot chocolate she was used to having.

Zoe was watching her closely. "I found some peppermint schnapps in the back pantry. Thought it sounded good."

Riley took a sip. It was amazing. "Wow, I think I like it better than the butterscotch and I didn't think that was possible."

Zoe sipped from her own cup. "Mm, it is good. Reminds me of Christmas."

Riley laughed.

"What?"

"That reminds me of Phoenix. He said he liked it up here because it smells like Christmas."

Zoe seemed amused. "It does smell like Christmas."

"That it does."

"He's a cute little guy," Zoe said. "Very perceptive."

"Mm, yes." Riley sipped some more.

"You don't have children?"

Riley felt the pang in her chest and lowered her mug. "No."

Zoe seemed to pick up on her change in mood.

"I'm sorry, I'm prying. It's just…you're so good with Phoenix. Seems like you should have children of your own."

"I came close once," Riley said softly, her mind fleeting over the memory.

"What happened?"

"My partner at the time suddenly decided to end things between us and the adoption fell through."

"Oh. I'm sorry."

Riley brought the cup to her mouth once again but couldn't bring herself to drink. "Yeah, it was a very difficult time. I lost her and the baby at the same time. Completely upended my life."

"And you never tried again? To adopt?"

Riley lowered the mug but couldn't meet her gaze. "No. It was just too hard to go through it all again. We had…before the last attempt we'd been promised a little boy. We had everything ready. Everything. And the day of the birth, the mother takes one look at him and changes her mind. She decided to keep him."

"That must've been really hard."

"It was. We were devastated. Holly, my partner, went into a depression. And I honestly don't think she was ever okay after that. Not even when we tried again. She'd just…changed. So when we were close the second time she suddenly announces she's in love with her personal trainer and she's leaving me to go start a new life, that she didn't want the baby. And that was…it."

"I'm so sorry, Riley."

"Yeah, well what are you gonna do, you know? That's life."

"Can you not…have children on your own?"

Riley shook her head. "I can't and Holly…didn't want to. She preferred adoption."

"Maybe you should try again. To adopt."

Riley set down her mug and ran her hands through her hair. She sighed and stared into the fire.

"I don't think I have the strength. And honestly, I don't want to do it alone. I want…a partner. A wife. A family."

"And you haven't met anyone since?"

Riley laughed. "Everything sounds so simple when you say it."

"Maybe you're making things harder than they need to be."

Riley propped her elbow on the back of the couch and leaned on her hand. Zoe was looking at her so innocently.

"You have no idea what it's like to fall for a woman. It's not a walk in the park and it's not something you recover from lightly."

"You presume to know more about me than you do."

Riley raised an eyebrow. "You've fallen for a woman before?"

"Well, no, but—"

Riley laughed.

"No, but I can understand how powerful it must be."

"And how can you possibly understand that?"

"Because I—" She shook her head.

Riley waited.

"Just in being with you these past couple of days I can sort of understand it."

Riley swallowed. Her skin heated. "Sort of understand it?"

"Yes, I—" But she glanced away.

"You what?" Riley saw the blush creep up her neck to her cheeks and she wondered if her own rivaled it. "Zoe?"

"I just can understand it, okay?"

Riley saw the pulse jumping in her neck, and the urge to rest her lips there to feel it nearly floored her.

"Zoe, are you...having feelings?"

Zoe looked down at her coffee mug in her lap. "I don't know." She inhaled sharply and looked up at Riley. "You're just...really incredible. So nice. And, well...beautiful."

Riley's heart pounded in her ears.

"But I'm not going to do anything," Zoe said quickly. "I mean I know I'm a guest here and a virtual stranger and I'm not like that, you know. I would never try to seduce you or anything like that and—"

"Zoe," Riley said.

"I mean that would be crazy and inappropriate and—"

"Zoe."

She stopped.

"Just relax, okay?"

Zoe took in a shaky breath. "Okay."

"Just breathe."

"I'm trying."

"Yeah, I'm finding it a little difficult myself."

"You are?"

"Yes."

"Why?"

"I think you know why."

Zoe swallowed and turned back toward the fire. "I'm not sure what's happening. I'm—feeling a little strange."

"It's called mutual attraction."

Zoe rang her hands around her coffee mug.

"And it's perfectly natural. You haven't done anything wrong."

"I feel so—I don't know. This is your home. I'm your guest."

"You're human. A woman. A very intriguing, intelligent, beautiful woman. There's nothing wrong with how you're feeling."

She laughed. "Easy for you to say. You've felt this way before."

"Actually, I haven't. Not like this. Not so strongly so quickly."

Zoe met her gaze. The whiskey embers were ablaze in the reflection of the fire. She touched her throat as if she were at a loss for words.

Riley inched closer, reached, out and took her hand.

"Just relax."

"I don't think I can. It's like every look you give me, every move you make, I'm keen to. Like my senses are wide open and taking you in."

Riley brought her hand to her mouth and lightly kissed her knuckles. Then she did the same to her inner wrist and palm, and Zoe struggled for breath as her eyes widened and then narrowed with obvious desire.

"Riley," she whispered. She squeezed her legs together as if the pressure between them was getting to her. Riley desperately wanted to help her with that, but she refrained and released her hand. Instead, she stroked her cheek.

"It's okay," she said.

"It's not," she said with a laugh. "You don't know what you're doing to me."

Riley smiled. "Oh, I do. But I'll stop."

"Yes, please do—I can't—I don't know what to do."

"You don't have to do anything."

She exhaled and placed her mug on the coffee table. Then she rubbed her palms on her jeans and stood. She looked frantic.

"Zoe, you don't have to do anything."

"But I want to, Riley. I really, really want to. That's why I have to leave for now, okay?"

"Zoe—"

"No, please. I need to go to my room."

She turned and raced off through the kitchen and down the hall. Riley sat and listened as she pulled her door closed.

CHAPTER TWENTY-TWO

Zoe put down the paperback and rubbed her eyes. She'd read the same page four times and still couldn't comprehend a thing. It was time to give up.

She tossed the book aside and stood to stretch. The clock next to the bed read ten. She'd been in her room for hours after having run from Riley to hide her growing emotions. Riley had knocked on her door once, simply to ask if she was hungry for dinner. Zoe had politely declined and Riley had let her be. Now it was after dark and the wind was howling and the snow no doubt ready to begin falling once again. She hugged herself in her flannel pants and long-sleeved shirt and opened her door carefully. She stepped into the hall but saw only the small sink light in the kitchen was illuminated. She wondered if Riley had gone to bed or if she was reading by the fire.

The image struck her and warmed her throughout, and she realized the rising tide of desire she'd felt earlier hadn't abated. It had just waited.

She used the restroom and then checked herself in the mirror. She freed her hair from the ponytail and finger combed it, then washed her face and brushed her teeth. Riley had kindly provided everything she needed, even the new toothbrush.

She is kind. So very kind.

Zoe pressed her palms to her face and tried to recall ever feeling this way about anyone. She couldn't.

She extinguished the light and walked through the kitchen to the living room. The fire was burning but dying slowly. There was no sign of Riley.

Zoe glanced up toward her loft and saw a soft light aglow. She decided to climb the stairs to apologize for hiding. She should've at least had dinner with her and tried to better explain. After all she could control herself and her feelings. Couldn't she?

She slowly climbed the stairs and entered the loft. She stopped as Riley lowered the hardback book she'd been reading.

"Hi," Zoe said, a little unsure of herself.

Riley brushed her hair back from her shoulder and sat up. The white satin pajamas she had on shimmered in the light. And the room smelled glorious, just as she did. Zoe had to fight to remain standing upright.

"Hi. How are you feeling?"

"A little better I think."

Riley smiled softly. "Good, I'm glad." She seemed to wait a moment, like she was waiting for Zoe to say something more before she spoke again. "Are you hungry? Can I make you something?"

"No, I—" She stopped, trying to get control of herself. "No thanks. I'm not hungry." It was true, she wasn't hungry. She was ravenous. But not for food.

Oh God.

She palmed her forehead, once again battling for control.

"I couldn't sleep, so I thought I'd check on you."

Riley set the book aside on the nightstand. "Oh."

"Actually, that's a lie. I didn't even try to sleep because I knew that I couldn't. I was trying to read but couldn't do that either."

Riley sat in silence, watching her closely.

"Well, I think we have something in common then. Because I've been having trouble reading as well." She motioned toward the book. "I couldn't tell you what that book was about to save my life." She smirked and Zoe's heart rate tripled.

God, she is...sexy. Yes, that's the word. Riley is sexy.

Zoe laughed and it sounded ridiculous to her own ears. She began to fidget with her hands.

"What should we do then?" Zoe asked, both scared and exhilarated at the possible scenarios of an answer.

"I don't know, what would you like to do?"

It could've been an innocent question. A polite one a hostess asked their guest. But Zoe knew it was anything but innocent. She could see it in her fiery green eyes, the brush of color on her cheeks. The way she licked her lips and pulled her legs up to rest her arms on them.

Or maybe that was all in her head. Maybe that was her hypersensitivity when it came to Riley.

But it didn't matter. She felt how she felt so she answered the way she hoped Riley wanted her to.

"I want to get in the bed with you."

Riley blinked. Then bit her lower lip. "Are you sure? It may be difficult to sleep."

"I'm not thinking about sleep."

Riley watched her. And when she spoke her voice was strained. "What are you thinking about then?"

Zoe swallowed the ball in her throat. "I'm thinking about what you said, about what it feels like to fall for a woman. I want to know what that feels like. What it really feels like. Not just what I've been imagining in my head."

"You been imagining it?"

"Yes," Zoe whispered. "From the second I laid eyes on you."

Riley climbed from the bed. She walked to Zoe slowly, eyes trained on hers, and reached out for her hand. She kissed it softly and then led her to the bed where she stood eye to eye with her.

"Are you sure this is what you want?" she asked again.

Zoe nodded. "Are you sure this is okay with you?"

Riley caressed her face. "Oh, yes, Zoe. It is."

Zoe trembled beneath her touch as Riley skimmed her thumb across her lips.

"The most exquisite lips I've ever seen," Riley whispered. "You are beautiful, Zoe."

And she dipped her head and kissed her, pressing her mouth to hers so softly, so carefully, Zoe felt like she'd float away in bliss.

And just when she thought she might drift away completely, Riley turned her and eased her down onto the bed and kissed her so deeply and so thoroughly that there could be no mistaking where she was or what was happening.

Chapter Twenty-three

Riley drank from her until she felt her head spin and her heart pound like it was about to explode into a million pieces. Breathless, she drew away only to have Zoe grip her pajamas and come up off the bed after her. Like they were magnets that couldn't be parted.

"Don't—" Zoe pleaded.

"Shh, I'm not going anywhere." Riley pulled back the covers and encouraged her to climb beneath them. When she was settled, Riley leaned over her, stroking her face. They were both breathing hard, their skin flushed.

"You kiss like you're—" Zoe started.

"Like what?"

"Like you're dying. Like it's the last thing you're ever going to get to do."

Riley stared into her eyes. "Oh, there's no way I'm dying now. Not after I've tasted you." She smiled and touched her lip. "You're just too good. Too savory."

She kissed her again, caught up in the amazement that she was beneath her mouth, in her bed, in her arms. And she hadn't been exaggerating about her taste. She was absolutely delicious, like the sweetest of elixirs. There was no way a human being could concoct anything so good. No way. Zoe was heaven sent.

"Mm, you are too," Zoe breathed as Riley attacked her neck. "So soft and slick."

Riley laughed into her skin. "You have no idea."

Zoe clawed at her back as Riley hit a particularly sensitive spot. "Wha? What do you mean?" She arched into her as Riley answered her with a light nibble beneath her ear.

"Oh, God, Riley, it feels so good. How can anything feel this good?" She began to writhe as Riley moved lower, grazing her teeth along the column of her neck. "I feel—oh God." She lifted her hips. "I feel it——-"

Riley stopped and lowered her hand between her legs. "Here?" She pressed against the heat of her pants and Zoe came up off the bed.

"Yes!"

Riley nibbled her ear lobe. "I think I can help you with that."

Zoe closed her eyes and held her forehead. "This is crazy. I'm about to go out of my mind I want you to touch me so badly."

"Shh, just relax. I'm not going anywhere, okay. We have all night."

"Oh God, I don't think I can take this all night. I'll have a heart attack for sure."

Riley laughed. "No, you won't. I'll make sure."

Zoe opened her eyes. "How can you be sure?"

"Because I'm enjoying myself way too much. I want you with me every single second to enjoy this with me. I promise I won't let anything happen to you."

Zoe swallowed. "Okay."

"Now relax," Riley encouraged her.

Zoe nodded and took a deep breath and Riley slowly drew her hand up to her waistband and slid it inside. Zoe hissed as Riley found her all wet and warm.

"Jesus," Riley croaked, the sensation immediately triggering her own response between her legs.

Zoe moaned and opened her eyes. She locked her gaze with Riley's and whispered, "Oh, God yes, Riley." And she began to move her hips in unison with Riley's hand. "Riley, yes. Oh God."

Riley closed her own eyes, nearly taken away by the sounds of her pleasure and the movement of her body beneath her hand. She was just about to tell her so when the room darkened and Zoe stilled beneath her.

Riley opened her eyes. "What? What is it?"

"The light went out," Zoe said.

Riley searched the dark room, confused.

Zoe stiffened. "I think the lights went out downstairs too."

Riley turned to stare out over the vaulted ceiling. She could no longer see the glow of light from the kitchen sink.

"It's the storm," she said. But Zoe grabbed her by the wrist. "Riley, I'm scared."

Riley gently removed her hand from her pants and pulled her closer. "It's just a power outage from the storm. Everything is okay."

"I don't think so," Zoe said. "What if it's him?"

"It's not." Riley brushed her hair from her cheek. "This happens in this kind of weather. I just need to go turn on the generator."

"No!"

"Zoe, I—"

"Not tonight. Please. Do it tomorrow in the light. We'll be warm for tonight, right? We have the fire and you have candles."

"But what if it's just a breaker? All I need to do is go check."

"No!" She clung to her. "Please don't. Not now, not tonight. Stay with me."

Riley rested her hand on her chest and felt her heart racing. She was obviously terrified. "Okay. I'll stay in."

"Thank you."

"But first thing tomorrow I'm going to go check."

She felt Zoe nod. "Okay."

Riley settled down next to her and held her close. The wind kicked up outside and howled through the trees.

"Riley?" Zoe asked after a few quiet moments.

"Yes?"

"Do you have a gun?"

Chapter Twenty-four

Zoe paced in front of the fireplace, feeling just as cold and hollow as the empty hearth. She checked her watch and bit at a nail. Riley had been checking on the power for fifteen minutes now and she could no longer hear her moving around in the basement. Nerves on edge, she walked to the stairs that led down below and waited, listening for a sound.

"Riley? You down there?"

She strained to hear an answer, but there was none. Her heart careened in her chest. Where was she? What could she possibly be doing?

"Riley?"

She gave up and paced near the kitchen. A corner curio cabinet caught her eye behind the kitchen table. She hadn't paid it or its contents much mind before, but now she saw something that interested her. She crossed to it and opened the glass front door. Then she stood on her tiptoes and reached up for what she was after. She touched the cold metal with her fingertips and easily pulled the item from its stand. She brought it down in front of her and held it with both hands. Her breath quickened as she stared at the revolver.

"Careful," Riley said from behind, startling her. "She's old but she still works."

"Sorry, I—where have you been?"

Riley walked toward her in her stocking feet, carrying her boots in her hand. She deposited them by the back door and slid out of her coat.

"I went outside to have a look around."

"Alone?"

Riley gently took the gun. "Yes, alone," she said softly. "And I came back safely, so we won't be needing this." She put the gun back on its stand and closed the cabinet. "And you'll be glad to know I found nothing suspicious."

"Nothing?"

Riley held her hands. "Nothing. Just the howling wind and the blowing snow."

"What about the power?" Riley's words should have comforted her but they didn't.

Riley scratched her head. "That I can't figure out. Must be a line down somewhere from the storm."

Zoe walked away from her and hugged herself against the chill that had just swept over her.

It could still be him. He could've found her. How, she didn't know. But then again how had he done any of what he'd done thus far? He seemed to be able to do anything.

"It's nothing, Zoe, honestly."

"You don't know," Zoe said. "You don't know."

"I do know. It's just an outage from the storm. It happens all the time."

Zoe looked at her. "But you've even said yourself you've never been here in the snow before. So how would you know?"

Riley opened her mouth to speak but then seemed to change her mind. "I just know, okay? It's common sense when these kind of things are concerned." She held her hands. "Now why don't you come sit down and I'll get the fire going and get us something to eat?"

"How? We have no power."

"I'm pretty resourceful."

"What about the generator?"

"I think we should wait and use it at night. I'm not sure how long we'll need it for and I only have so much fuel."

Zoe felt a tremble run through her as she imagined them stuck in the cabin with no power for days on end.

"When are your friends coming back?"

"They are supposed to come Saturday."

"Supposed to?"

"We'll have to wait and see what the storm brings."

Zoe felt her eyes widen. Riley quickly led her to the couch and eased her down. "We'll be fine. We have plenty of supplies."

"What about the perishables? They'll spoil."

Riley smiled and touched her face. "I'm going to put them in a cooler and pack it with snow and leave it on the deck."

"Oh."

"Now, will you relax a little? Hm? Everything is fine."

Zoe wanted to shake her head, to argue even. But she had no ground to stand on. Everything Riley said made sense. Even if she didn't feel it in her gut.

"I think," Riley said, stroking her cheek, "that maybe you're too much on edge because of what you've been through."

Zoe swallowed and stilled her hand. Riley was trying to politely tell her that she was paranoid. Great.

"Hey," Riley said. But Zoe pulled away.

"I'm not imagining this," she said.

"I'm not saying you are."

Zoe hugged her knees to her chest. Riley watched her for a few moments and then rose. "I'm going to take care of the food and then take care of us."

"You don't have to," Zoe said. "Take care of me."

"I don't mind."

"No, really, I don't want anything. Not right now."

"Okay." Riley left her and headed for the kitchen. Zoe stared out the window at the vast white wonderland wondering how long it would be before the man appeared in front of the glass, wicked grin on his face. She turned to look at the gun again tucked away in its cabinet. Hopefully, he wouldn't appear before she had the chance to get that gun.

Chapter Twenty-five

Riley pulled on her coat, careful to keep quiet as to not wake Zoe on the couch. She'd fallen asleep attempting to read, and Riley had quickly covered her with a throw and tossed in another log to keep her warm.

She descended the stairs to the basement just as quietly and pulled open the garage door. They were already running a little low on firewood upstairs, and the sun would be setting soon. She thought it best to try to chop some before nightfall. Plus, it gave her something to do. Zoe had been distant for most of the day and it was beginning to bother her. She wasn't sure what she'd done wrong, and she was really concerned that Zoe seemed to be so scared. There just didn't seem to be a way to qualm her worries and that left her feeling helpless.

She removed the tarp from the wood pile and began chopping some wood. The exercise felt good, and she loved how the cold air stung her lungs as she inhaled. Soon, she'd shed her coat and was working up a good sweat. She was so engrossed in what she was doing she almost didn't hear the car pull alongside on the rode behind her.

Wiping sweat from her brow, she turned and focused on the vehicle. For a split second she'd thought it might be Elise and Keira, surprising her with an early arrival. But that thought was soon dashed as she took in the large navy blue SUV sitting idle, plumes of exhaust spilling into the chilled air from the tailpipe. The driver's window eased down, and a hand waved at her.

She approached slowly, with Zoe's worries in her mind, but then felt ridiculous. She halted when the door opened and a man stepped out, dressed in camo style winter garb. He smiled at her and waved again.

"Hi," he said, rubbing his hands together. He turned back to the vehicle and spoke to someone. Then a dog climbed down from the driver's seat and promptly began sniffing the powdery snow for a place to relieve itself.

"Can I help you?" Riley said. The man tugged on his Cabela's ball cap.

"No, I think we're good. She just needed a break."

Riley knelt to pet her. "She's pretty."

Riley straightened and noted which direction his SUV was pointed. He was headed up not down. Curious.

"You headed up to your place?" Riley asked.

"Yeah." The man exhaled like he was tired. "Going up to a buddy's cabin. Gonna hunt for some wild turkey."

Riley eyed the dog. "She doesn't look much like the hunting dog type."

The man laughed. "You'd be surprised. She can be tenacious."

The dog squatted and peed and then pulled on the lead, wanting to come to Riley again.

"Very pretty."

"Looks are deceiving," the man said with a chuckle. "I'm Don, by the way." He stuck out his hand. Riley took it.

"Riley."

"You up here hunting too?" he asked.

"Me? Oh no. Not into that."

"It's not for everyone." His gaze bypassed her to her cabin. "Gotta nice place there. A lot nicer than my buddy's place."

Riley looked back at her cabin and felt a little sense of pride. "She's coming along nicely."

He looked at her for a long moment and then smiled again. "Well, we better be off."

"Yeah, I need to get back inside before my friend sends out a search party."

The man's gaze focused beyond her as they heard a door close back at the cabin. He grinned. "I think you may be too late." He tugged on the dog's lead. "It was nice meeting you."

"You too."

He climbed in the truck and closed the door. Then, with one last wave, he drove off, leaving Riley waving after him.

"Who was that?" Zoe asked from behind. She was once again hugging herself, standing there without a coat or a hat.

"What are you doing? You'll freeze out here." Riley rested her hand on the small of her back and led her back toward the house.

"Who was that?"

"I don't know, just some guy."

Zoe stopped, eyes wide.

"He's fine. Just some hunter. Even had his dog with him."

"You talked to him?"

"Yes, I talked to him. He was nice. Just stopped on his way up to let his dog relieve herself."

"On his way up? I thought you said there weren't many cabins up beyond you?"

"There aren't."

Zoe shook her head.

"Zoe, come on. He was fine. He was even dressed like a hunter. All camoed out and everything."

"Yeah, because he's going to be hunting me."

"Honestly, Zoe, you need to calm down a little."

"Calm down? Riley, who comes up here to go hunting in the middle of a snowstorm?" Zoe's brow was raised and she crossed her arms and stuck out a foot as if waiting for answer.

"He had chains on his tires and there was a break in the storm."

"It's supposed to start up again isn't it?"

"Yes, but—"

"Again, I ask you, who goes hunting in the middle of a snowstorm?"

Riley had no answer. Not one that she knew would suffice. She didn't tell her it was a little late in the season for turkey hunting too. All that would do was scare her more.

Zoe seemed satisfied, but when she spoke her words reflected a sadness more than a satisfaction.

"Please don't ever tell me to calm down." She walked back toward the house without another word.

CHAPTER TWENTY-SIX

Zoe wiped a tear as she tossed some folded clothes into a plastic bag and zipped up her backpack. She was so hurt and frustrated that she could just scream. Nobody believed her or took her seriously. She'd thought she'd finally found someone in Riley, but it seemed she'd been wrong. Riley was just like everyone else, well-meaning though she may be.

She stood her backpack up on the bed and made sure everything was closed tight. Her tent and sleeping bag and other goods were back at the cabin, but she'd decided to leave them. After all, Riley was right. She couldn't survive there in this weather, and now she didn't even want to try. There was a mysterious hunter on the mountain who she knew in her gut didn't belong there. So, to hell with staying at her grandfather's cabin.

"Hi." There was a soft knock at the bedroom door.

Zoe turned and found Riley at the doorway, a look of sorrow on her face. "I just wanted to apologize—" She stepped into the room and her eyes fixed on the backpack and bag. "What are you doing?"

"Leaving."

Riley looked frantic. "Leaving? You can't leave. You'll freeze—"

"I'm not going back to the cabin. I'm going into town."

"Town?"

"If you'll take me."

"Zoe, I don't understand. I thought you were afraid to go—"

"I am. But there's no sense in staying here. You don't believe me and I'm in your way and—"

"Hey," Riley said, gently holding her shoulders. "You're not in my way and I do believe you. I just think—"

"I'm too paranoid. Right?"

"I think you could relax some, yes."

Zoe tried to shrug into her backpack. She nearly fell over.

Riley steadied her. "It's not an insult you know," she said. "Suggesting you relax. I'm just worried about your stress level. And this little mark right here."

She traced her fingertip down the center of Zoe's forehead where she was beginning to grow a permanent line.

Zoe softly pushed her hand away. "I'm fine."

"You're not and that little mark tells me so."

Zoe glanced away from her. The caring look she was giving her was too much to handle, too difficult to fight. Why did Riley have to be so irresistible? And so damn kind?

"Just take me into town, please."

Riley frowned. "I can't. It's snowing again. Supposed to snow all night and into tomorrow."

"You have chains for your Bronco. Don't you?"

"Zoe, I'm not trekking that mountain road out there in this. You saw those overhangs. It's too dangerous."

"What about the hunter then? He somehow made it."

Riley seemed to think. "Yeah, come to think of it I'm not sure how he did that. With all the fresh snow we've had the past two days it had to be tricky. Even with the break in the storm."

"Maybe he didn't just arrive," Zoe said. "Maybe he's been here a while already."

Zoe lifted her pack and stumbled a bit as she tried to move around Riley.

"Zoe, wait." Riley gripped the pack and carefully held her upper arm. Her eyes were ablaze with care and concern. "We can't go. Not now. It's too dangerous."

"Then when?"

"When it stops again and melts off a little. Three, maybe four days."

Zoe sighed and dropped her bag to the floor. "Then what now, Riley? Sit and wait, like sitting ducks?"

"No," Riley said with a soft chuckle. She touched her cheek, then her forehead. "We relax and enjoy this peaceful retreat."

"No," Zoe said. "We go downstairs and you show me how to use that gun."

Riley dropped her gaze and her hand. After a few seconds, she turned with a sigh and whispered, "Okay."

❖

Zoe stood hunched over in the snow, waiting at the patio railing. Riley emerged carrying the gun along with a box of bullets. The furrow to her brow indicated she was not happy about doing this.

"It's an old Smith and Wesson," she said by way of greeting. "I don't shoot it often."

"So it really does work?"

"Yes, it works." She came to stand next to Zoe and began loading the bullets in the chamber. "I like old guns, but I'm not very big on using them. Most of the time I hope I don't have to." She closed the revolver and handed it over the Zoe. "You ever shoot before?"

"No. I don't like guns."

Riley rubbed her brow. "Guess you really must be scared then."

"I am."

The wind kicked up and stung Zoe's face. She stared down at the gun, noted the six-inch barrel and the heavy feel of it in her palm. Her fingers felt cold, bordering on numb.

"Don't worry, it won't fire until you cock the trigger."

Carefully, Zoe held the gun in position, aiming it down into the vast valley of snowcapped trees below. She trembled. Riley came behind her and leaned into her, holding the gun with her.

"Relax and breathe," she whispered into her ear. "There's nothing to be afraid of."

Zoe closed her eyes and took in deep breaths.

"Okay, now open your eyes and gently squeeze the trigger. Don't pull, squeeze."

Zoe focused as best she could and steadied her hands in Riley's. She inhaled and squeezed the trigger. The gun fired and kicked but not as powerfully as she'd expected. In the distance, she heard bark crack and snow cascaded down from a tree.

"You're a good shot," Riley said.

"I wasn't aiming," Zoe admitted.

"Even better." Riley drew away from her. "Think you can shoot on your own now?"

Zoe nodded. "I think so."

Riley motioned for her to try. "This time try and aim for something and line your target up with the sight on the end of the barrel."

Zoe closed one eye and aimed for a neighboring tree. She pulled back on the trigger and steadied her grip. Then she inhaled and fired once again. She clipped the trunk of the tree, sending more snow flying.

"Not bad," Riley said.

"Try one more."

Zoe repeated the steps and shot again. This time she hit her mark almost dead center.

Riley laughed. "You didn't need me after all, did ya?"

"Guess not."

Riley smiled at her as the wind kicked up again. "Feel better?"

Zoe returned the smile. "Much."

They headed back inside and Riley held the door for her.

"Think you can relax now?"

Zoe thought for a second. "Only if you let me carry the gun around."

Riley laughed again. "I was afraid you were going to say something like that."

CHAPTER TWENTY-SEVEN

Riley fussed over the generator one more time and then kicked it.

"Damn." She hopped a little at the pain in her toe and cursed herself for being so stupid. "Why won't you work?"

She tried again, and miraculously, the generator rumbled to life and the light in the garage flickered on.

"Maybe I should kick things more often." She stood staring at the generator for a while, wanting to make sure it stayed on. After a few minutes, she felt satisfied and left it under the overhang of the patio and went back into the house through the garage.

She secured the garage door closed with a chain lock and wiped her hands on her jeans. Normally she wouldn't be so concerned over locking the garage door in a case like this, but she wanted Zoe to feel secure should she ask. She was already insisting on keeping the gun close at hand, as well as checking the weather on the radio every chance she got. Riley didn't want her to have to worry about anything else.

Riley killed the light and headed upstairs. Zoe was sitting by the fire, leaning against the stone hearth, stabbing at the logs with the fire poker. She looked beautiful in the firelight and for once even a little relaxed.

"You look cozy," Riley said, removing her coat. She hung it by the door and deposited her boots.

"I feel cozy," Zoe said with an easy grin. She turned slightly and held up a mug. "Thanks to the butterscotch schnapps."

"Oh, I see. Did you happen to make me one?"

"I did." She eyed the mug on the coffee table.

"Thank you," Riley said, picking it up and taking a sip. She joined Zoe by the fire.

"You got the generator working," Zoe said.

Riley glanced into the fire, all too aware of Zoe's glowing irises and shining shoulder length hair. "Finally, yes. Not sure what was wrong with it."

"Maybe it just needed a little love and affection."

Like me?

Riley shook the thought away.

"What about a kick?"

"You kicked it?"

Riley chuckled. "Uh-huh." She wiggled her toes. "Got the sore foot to prove it."

"Let me see," Zoe said. She patted Riley's leg, encouraging her to rest her foot on her lap.

Riley shook her head. "It's fine."

"No, seriously, let me see." Zoe gently grabbed her foot and straightened Riley's leg. She carefully began massaging the ball of her foot, mindful of her toes. Riley couldn't help but groan.

"See, I'm not going to hurt you."

"Promise?"

She smirked. "Now where does it hurt?"

"My big toe."

Zoe massaged upward toward her toe and when Riley winced, she stopped and removed her sock.

"Here?" she asked, examining her.

"Uh-huh."

"Can you bend it?"

Riley moved it. "Yeah. It's not broken."

"Just bruised. You should probably ice it."

"Yeah, no thanks." She drew her foot away and slid into her sock.

"Stubborn."

"No, just cold enough already, thanks."

"Oh, so you're a wimp."

"No," Riley said, louder than she'd intended.

Zoe laughed. "Oh, I think I hit a nerve."

"Whatever."

Riley shifted a little to swat her in the arm, but the movement hurt her toe and she winced again, which caused Zoe to laugh even harder.

"Serves you right," she said, swatting her back with a throw pillow.

"Quit," Riley said, shielding herself.

"Here, at least elevate your foot on this pillow." She propped Riley's foot up and gave her another grin. "Wuss."

Riley narrowed her eyes. "You're lucky I'm injured."

"Yeah, I'm sure I am. You being so dangerous and all."

"Maybe I am. Maybe I'm your stalker."

"Oh really? It's you? After all this time?"

"Hey, it could be."

"Right." Her laughter died. "No, I know it's not you."

"How do you know?"

"Other than the million obvious reasons?"

"Yes."

"Because you wouldn't ever do anything to hurt me."

"How do you know that?"

"By the way you look at me." She looked into the fire then, as if she'd said too much. "No one has ever looked at me the way you do."

Riley swallowed hard, watched her quietly. "You're right," she said. "I'd never hurt you."

"Think the hunter would?" Zoe met her gaze once again.

Riley shook her head. "No, I don't."

"How can you be so sure?"

"I didn't get that vibe from him."

"You ever been around someone with a killer vibe?" Zoe asked.

"Not that I know of."

"Then how do you know?"

Riley shrugged. "I think it was the way he was with his dog. He cared about her. He was good with her. You could tell. And I generally trust people who are good with animals."

"You ever met someone who wasn't?"

"Yes, and I steered clear."

Zoe nodded. "Me too." She sipped her drink. "Why don't you have a dog?"

Riley focused on her mug of steaming hot chocolate. "I did."

"Oh, did it…you know, die? I'm sorry."

"No. He's fine. He's with my ex. She insisted on taking him and I honestly just didn't want the fight."

"Do you ever get to see him?"

"No."

"She doesn't let you?"

"No, that's not it."

"Then why don't you see him? Don't you want to?"

Riley swallowed. She rubbed her brow. "It's not him that I can't bear seeing."

"Oh."

Riley exhaled and tried to stand. Zoe stopped her however, with a gentle touch of her hand. "Please, don't go. Sit with me a while longer."

Riley eased back down and Zoe smiled. "Thanks."

After a few moments of silence, Zoe finally spoke. "You know, if you ask me, I'd say the dog got the shit end of the deal." She looked at Riley and smirked once again.

Riley laughed. Laughed really hard.

And man, did it feel good.

CHAPTER TWENTY-EIGHT

Zoe awoke with a start, sitting straight up in bed. Her heart pounded in her chest, and she fumbled for the light, but the lamp wouldn't turn on. Hurriedly, she scrambled for the flashlight she'd left on the night table and switched it on. She searched the bedroom but found it empty. Dark. Outside, the wind blew against the cabin, fierce and unforgiving.

She climbed from the bed and tried the light switch. Nothing. Oh God.

With her heart now in her ears, she padded carefully into the hallway and swung the flashlight beam into the kitchen. The sink light. It was off as well. She tried the switch there. Nothing.

She hurried into the living room, saw the dying fire, and whispered up the stairs for Riley. She got no response.

She swung the beam of light toward the back door and nearly sighed when she saw it still closed and bolted. At least that was still secure.

Quietly, she began to ascend the spiral staircase, one agonizing step at a time. When she reached the top, she aimed the flashlight at Riley's bed. A lump was under the covers and she hurried to it, grateful to see Riley's black hair spilling out onto a pillow.

"Riley," she whispered.

"Wha?"

"Riley, wake up." She shook her shoulder, then took a moment to look over her own to make sure no one had followed her up the stairs.

"Riley."

"Okay, I'm up." Riley rolled over and shielded her eyes from the flashlight. "What's wrong?"

Zoe shifted the light away from her and sat on the bed. "The lights are out."

Riley sat up, tried to turn on her lamp. It didn't work.

"It's probably just the generator. No big deal."

"What if it isn't? I mean, what if it is a big deal?"

Riley ran her hand through her hair and rubbed her face. "You're not going to let this go are you?"

Zoe shook her head. "I can't."

"Okay, I'll get up." She crawled from the bed and crossed to her closet where she slipped into her robe.

"Shouldn't you change, you know, in case there's trouble?"

Riley sighed. "Okay." She began to undress, and Zoe turned away and focused on the gun on the bedside table. Riley had refused to let her sleep with it, afraid she'd shoot herself, so Zoe had insisted she take it upstairs with her. Now Zoe wanted it more than ever, to keep in her pocket and to sleep with by her bed.

Riley finished dressing and rounded the bed. She held out her hand for the flashlight. Zoe handed it over and then grabbed the gun.

"Don't forget this."

Riley eyed her for a second and then took it, shoving it into the back of her jeans. Then they both descended the stairs and headed for the door where they stepped into their boots.

"You're coming with me?" Riley asked, sounding surprised.

"Yes." There was no way she was waiting upstairs alone, sans gun, in the pitch-black, waiting for Riley to give her the all clear.

"Suit yourself."

They descended the basement stairs and Riley unlocked and opened the door leading to the garage. The dark room was silent with the strong smell of gasoline. It was also freezing.

Riley walked outside to the quiet generator and knelt. She handed the flashlight over to Zoe and then began fumbling with the machine.

"What the hell?" She held up her hand and sniffed. "What the hell?" She backed away and lifted her foot to examine the bottom of her shoe. Zoe shined the spotlight on the ground and saw the reflection of liquid pooled around the generator.

"Gas?" Zoe asked.

"How in the hell did that happen?" Riley knelt again and scrutinized the tank. "Damn thing's leaking."

Zoe hugged herself from an internal chill that was far stronger than the one being blown in by the wind.

"Someone punctured it?"

"I don't think so."

"But they could have. They could've crawled under this overhang and—"

Riley shook her head. "I don't think so, Zoe. I think this damn thing is just old. Probably why it's been giving me trouble."

"But someone could've—"

"But why, Zoe? To do this? And only this? Why not come upstairs and kill us?"

"Maybe—"

"No." Riley kicked the generator. "Ow, damn it." She grabbed her foot. "Enough of the stalker talk, okay? For tonight anyway? Please?"

Zoe nodded, defeated.

"Can we at least…"

Riley sighed. "Yes?"

"Double lock the garage since the generator isn't working? It's not like we'll have to come back out and check it tonight."

"Sure." Riley closed and double locked the garage door with another set of chains and they headed back up into the cabin.

Then Riley said good night to her and went to bed alone, leaving Zoe downstairs, heart still pounding in her ears.

CHAPTER TWENTY-NINE

Riley finished clearing the patio as best she could and then went down around the back to start in on the drive in front of the garage door. Snow was falling in light flurries, kissing her face with delicate teases of ice and the wind was blowing in sporadic gusts, blowing more snow from the treetops. Though it was a storm, it was a beautiful sight to behold, especially in the early light of dawn.

Riley trudged down to the garage and halted, snow shovel in hand. She blinked a few times to be sure she was seeing correctly. There before her, in the heavy snow, were tracks leading to and from the garage door. The recent snowfall had nearly covered them, but they were still visible and unmistakable.

Riley examined them next to her own print. They were boot prints, larger than her own. She glanced hurriedly around, convinced she was mistaken. These were just prints from the night before when she and Zoe had come out to check the generator. But no, they couldn't be. They were too big and they were the only prints left in the snow. The ones that belonged to her and Zoe had long been covered from the continued snowfall in the night. Her heart rate kicked up at the impossibility of it. There was no way. It couldn't be.

She dropped the shovel and rounded the house. She hurried inside and ran to the basement stairs. She scrambled down them and burst into the garage and ran to the door in the dark. She fumbled with the locks and released the chains and pulled open the door. The light spilled in and she inhaled a huge breath of cold air.

No one had been inside the garage. The locks and chains had been in place. Thank God.

She still looked around frantically, feeling overwhelmed and violated regardless. She walked back out to the generator and examined it in the pale morning light but couldn't make out a thing. Then, thinking of Zoe, she closed and locked the garage again and ran back upstairs. She hurried down the hallway to Zoe's room and cracked open the door. She was sound asleep in her bed, flashlight in hand. Riley pulled the door closed and then climbed the stairs to her room. She sat on her bed and reached for the gun. She held it in her hand for a long time before she opened the barrel. Then she opened the nightstand drawer and pulled out the box of bullets. She loaded the gun she'd thought unnecessary and silly, then secured the barrel and slid the gun into the back of her jeans.

She rose and walked to the stairs where she slowly descended, feeling truly afraid for the first time in her life.

"You're awful quiet," Zoe said as they finished breakfast. "Any luck with the generator?"

"No. But I need to go work on it some more." Truth was, the generator was the last thing on her mind. First and foremost was who was doing this and why, and second was how she was going to tell Zoe without her freaking out.

Should she tell her?

Just how badly would she freak out?

She had to tell her. They were in danger.

"I don't want to alarm you, but the storm is going to ease up a bit today and I think we should try to make it down in the Bronco."

"Why would that alarm me?"

"Because it's sooner than we talked about."

"Oh. Well, the sooner the better as far as I'm concerned."

Riley sipped her juice and contemplated.

"What is it?" Zoe asked. "Something's wrong. I can tell."

Riley focused out the window beyond them. "I think you were right about the generator last night."

"What?" Zoe stood, palms on the table.

"I found footprints. Early this morning. Footprints other than ours."

"Oh, my God." Zoe clutched her heart. "Oh, my God."

Riley stood with her and tried to calm her down. "I checked the whole house. No one is in here. We're safe."

"Why didn't you tell me? Safe? You really think we're safe? Are you insane?"

She pushed away from the table and headed for the hallway. "We have to go. We have to go now."

"Zoe, it's storming."

"I don't care! I'm leaving now!"

Riley chased her. "Zoe, please calm down. We have to be calm about this, make good decisions."

Zoe spun and faced off with her. "Look, I'm packing up and I'm leaving. You coming? Or are you staying? Either way, I'm going."

She turned and started throwing clothes into her pack. Riley left her, feeling helpless, and went to do the same, unsure about the decision to leave in the storm, unsure about everything.

CHAPTER THIRTY

Zoe opened the passenger door to the Bronco and slung her backpack inside. She climbed in and buckled her seat belt, waiting anxiously for Riley to do the same. They'd locked up the entire house and were ready to go. Riley was moving a little slower than she liked.

At last Riley finished clearing the snow from the vehicle and climbed in next to her. She'd insisted on packing up most everything, including the cooler, and the back was nearly full. While Zoe, on the other hand, thought their lives were a little more important than loading up the perishables.

"Are you finally ready?" Zoe asked as Riley buckled her seat belt.

"Yes, Zoe. I'm finally ready."

"I'm sorry, I just don't see the point in packing up everything. I'm a little more concerned for our lives."

"I just don't want to come back to a cabin full of rotten food and trash. It will attract animals—"

"Screw that, Riley. We need to go."

"Fine!" Riley threw up her hands.

"I don't get it. Why aren't you scared?"

"I am, Zoe. I'm just trying to be calm and rational. To me, it doesn't make sense that somebody would go to all that trouble in the storm just to mess with the generator. I mean, why not mess with us? With you?"

"So what, you think they just did it for fun?"

Riley sighed. She fished out her keys and stuck them in the ignition. "No. But I've been wondering if someone was trying to help. Like maybe the hunter. Maybe he smelled the gas and didn't want to wake us, so he tried to fix it or something."

She turned the key. Nothing happened.

"Oh, right. Because he's just a random good Samaritan out checking on his neighbors in a snowstorm."

Riley grimaced and tried the ignition again. Nothing.

Zoe felt her mouth go dry. "Oh, no. He messed with the Bronco, didn't he?"

Riley tried again. Nothing. No noise, no clicking, nothing.

"Fuck!" She banged her fist on the steering wheel. "Fuck, fuck, fuck!"

"Oh, my God." Zoe grabbed her chest, her breathing suddenly labored. "We're trapped. We're stuck here, Riley."

Riley popped the hood and threw open her door. She scrambled out and cursed as she looked under the hood. Zoe climbed out after her and joined her. Wires were strewn everywhere, slit and cut.

"Oh, my God," Zoe let out. Tears filled her eyes.

Riley slammed down the hood.

Behind them, they heard a vehicle approach, crunching up onto the side drive. Zoe lost it, her heart damn near pounding out of her chest.

"Oh, my God, he's here. He's here!"

The dark SUV parked and the driver's door opened. A man climbed out and waved, tugging his cap down low.

"Afternoon," he said.

Zoe clung to Riley, tugging on her. "We have to get inside. Riley, we have to go!"

Riley stood ramrod still. "Shh, I want to see what he says," she whispered. "I have the gun in my pocket."

Zoe wanted to scream at her, beg her, yank on her, but fear took over and she froze. The man approached. He was wearing white camo clothes and thick boots. His breath came out in puffs and his cheeks were red with chill.

"Riley, right?" he said.

"Right," Riley answered.

He smiled. "I just came by to let you know that the trail down is now impassable. I just spent two hours digging my SUV out trying to get down."

"That's bad news," Riley said. "We were just headed down ourselves."

A dog barked from inside the vehicle and the man stopped his approach. "I was hoping with the break in the storm, I could make it down, but no dice." He motioned toward their Bronco. "You having car trouble?"

"Yeah," Riley glanced back at the Bronco. "I guess you could say that."

"Just as well, you won't make it down."

"I would've liked to try."

"I hear ya."

"Now, we have to unload everything," Riley said with a slight laugh.

"You need any help?" He took a couple of steps toward them.

"No!" Zoe said. "We're fine."

He froze. "You sure? I got nothing better to do."

"We're sure," Zoe said. "You can go." She clung to Riley, imagining the man pulling a gun out from his heavy-looking coat at any second. Or a large knife. Or both. She just wanted him to leave.

"I think we got it," Riley said. "But thanks."

The man stood still for a moment, examining them, then tugged on the bill of his cap and said, "Okay, then. Best of luck to you."

"You as well," Riley said.

He nodded and turned to go but paused and faced them again.

"Say, you two wouldn't happen to know anyone staying in that old abandoned cabin would you?"

Zoe squeezed Riley's arm so hard her hand hurt.

"No, why do you ask?" Riley said.

"No reason. Just, uh, keeping my eye out for someone." He smiled, tugged on his cap again, and walked away. He climbed in his vehicle and went back up the mountain trail.

Zoe trembled as she watched him go. "That's him, that has to be him."

"Did you recognize him?" Riley asked.

"I couldn't make out his face well enough. Why did you keep talking to him?"

"I wanted to see what he would say. See if he would give himself away."

Zoe hugged herself. "He said more than enough. Do you believe me now?"

Riley met her gaze. "Yes, Zoe, I believe you."

"What are we going to do?"

Riley stared out at the road, her gaze following the man's trail. "We're going to unpack and hunker down. It's all we can do."

Zoe pushed out a long, shaky, breath. "I was afraid you were going to say that."

CHAPTER THIRTY-ONE

Riley glanced down at her phone, saw that there was no signal, and tossed it on the coffee table.

"No luck?" Zoe asked from her curled position beneath two blankets. They had a raging fire, but it only seemed to be keeping the living room warm. Their backs, which were to the kitchen area, were prone to get chilled without the blankets.

Riley shook her head.

"Do you usually get a signal up here?"

"Sometimes. It's hit or miss."

"What a time for it to miss." She pulled the blankets tighter as if her words had just chilled her worse than the cold.

Riley thought about agreeing, but she didn't want to feed into the fear that they were both now feeling. Someone had to stay calm, think things through. Zoe was ready to fight tooth and nail or run for the hills. Neither would be wise given their current situation. First of all, they wouldn't know exactly who to fight. Was their mysterious enemy the hunter? Or was it someone else? She was beginning to think like Zoe, that the hunter seemed very suspicious. The way he seemed to show up when there seemed to be no one else on the mountain. It was rather strange, considering she hadn't heard or seen another soul. She'd even stood out on the back patio the other evening and scanned the sky and the valley below for chimney smoke, but all she'd seen were snow-topped trees.

And if they chose to run, where would they go? They'd freeze to death before they reached help.

No, it was better to stay calm and try to work things through. For now, they were safe. They had shelter, a fireplace, food. To leave on foot would be disastrous.

Riley pulled her feet up and snuggled under her own blanket. Dusk had come and gone, and she'd tried calling for help a few times every hour. She also sent texts, hoping they got through, but there was no telling. All she could hope for was for Keira and Elise to become concerned at the silence and try to make it up at the first melt.

"Do Keira and Elise know about my…situation?"

"What do you mean?"

"Do they know I'm here?"

Riley felt herself flush, recalling the one conversation she'd had with Keira since Zoe's arrival at her cabin.

"Yes, I told them you were staying with me for a while."

She waited for Zoe to get upset at having being spoken about, but she didn't.

"Good," she said. "That means they were probably already worried at hearing that news, so maybe they'll come quickly now. Maybe they'll think I'm holding you captive or something."

Riley couldn't tell if she was joking or not. Her mood had changed significantly since nightfall. She'd gone from outwardly angry and frightened, to quiet and paranoid. She wouldn't even look out the large windows, for fear that the hunter would be standing there, watching them. She'd even asked Riley if they could cover the windows somehow. She didn't like being in a fishbowl. She thought it gave the perpetrator an edge.

Riley didn't disagree. She'd just said there was no way to cover such large windows and she'd encouraged her to go up to the loft where she couldn't be seen unless someone was in an extremely tall tree. So far, she'd declined, preferring to stay where she could react readily if someone tried to get in. But Riley wasn't sure how much longer either one of them could last. Though they were on high alert, their bodies were giving out, their eyelids growing heavy. Zoe kept closing her eyes and nodding her head. Riley fought doing the same.

"Zoe."

"Yes?" She opened her eyes.

"Let's go up to bed."

"Huh-uh."

"Come on, we're both falling asleep. We wouldn't be of any use if he came in right now anyway. Not if we're asleep. At least upstairs it puts some distance between us. Maybe we would hear him and could properly react before he got to us."

Zoe seemed to think. Then she turned and snuck a peek outside the big black windows. She turned back, face ashen.

"Okay."

"Go on up and I'll tend to the fire."

Zoe stood and hurried to the staircase, climbing carefully as Riley put in two more good-sized logs for the night. Hopefully, with the hot air rising, they'd be warm enough. Worst-case scenario, they'd have to snuggle. The thought of that gave her a little thrill of sorts and she cursed herself for reacting that way under such conditions. She couldn't help it though. Zoe was different. Unique. Even if her mind told her she couldn't react to her, her body had a mind of its own.

She stoked the fire and double-checked the locks and then walked up the stairs. Zoe was already under the covers, looking incredibly beautiful under her red duvet. Her hair was free from its ponytail, and it hung in shiny waves in the candlelight. Despite their circumstances, the romantic feel of the moment was not lost on her.

Riley slid out of her slippers and began to undress to change into her pajamas.

"Riley, don't. Stay dressed in case something happens."

Riley nodded and crawled under the covers. It was the least she could do to comfort her, and she honestly couldn't help but agree. Staying dressed was a good idea.

"Where's the gun?"

Riley grunted as she reached back and pulled it from the waistband of her jeans. She set it on the night table.

"Is it loaded?"

"Yes. Now try to get some sleep, okay?"

Zoe turned on her side and faced Riley. She reached out for her hand and held it.

"Is this okay?"

"Yes," Riley breathed. Nothing had ever felt more right.

"Good night."

"Good night, Zoe."

Riley closed her eyes and she realized, as a wave of heavy warmth washed over her, just how exhausted she was. Stress really did do a number on the human body. She hadn't been so tired in years. In no time at all, she was fast asleep.

Riley bolted upright in bed as an incredibly loud crash sounded from somewhere outside. And just when she didn't think it could get louder it did, and it went on for several seconds, almost to where she was thinking an avalanche was upon them. Next to her, Zoe jumped from the bed, eyes wide and seeking in the low candlelight.

"What was that?" she said, sounding panicked.

Riley stood, crossed to the window. "I don't know."

"Riley, what the *fuck* was that?"

"I don't know."

"It sounded like King Kong just rolled down the mountainside."

"Something big obviously fell somewhere."

Zoe joined her at the window. "See anything?"

"No." Riley turned and headed for the stairs.

"Where are you going?"

"To see what that was."

"No, don't. Not now."

"Zoe, I—"

"Fine, I'm going with you."

She grabbed the gun and her flashlight and followed her down the stairs to join her at the door to step into their boots and coats. When they were ready, she handed over the gun.

Riley took it and tucked it into her coat pocket and then unlocked the door and headed out into the snowy cold. The wind stung her skin as they descended the patio steps and began walking toward the drive. Zoe swung her flashlight back and forth in front of them, but the night was still. Quiet. Black.

"It sounded like it came from over there," Riley said. She headed right, to where the trail led down the mountain. But again, they saw nothing. Heard nothing.

Until…

Clamoring. Twigs snapping.

Riley froze and Zoe aimed the flashlight toward the noise, down the hill to their right. Riley drew the gun, cocked the trigger. Zoe was saying something to her. Again and again.

It wasn't until she almost made the decision to do it herself that she comprehended.

"Shoot! Shoot, Riley, shoot!"

Riley closed one eye, inhaled sharply and was about to squeeze the trigger, when a white dog burst out from the trees and lunged through the deep snow.

Riley lost her balance as she struggled to regain her focus. She took a couple of steps back, at first confused at what she was seeing. Then, as she blinked, she realized it was the white dog she'd seen with the hunter, and it was yipping as it came toward them.

"Riley!" Zoe said as she gripped her arm, fear still evident on her face.

"No, it's okay," Riley said, lowering the gun. "I know her. She won't hurt you."

The dog ambled up to them, tongue licking its lips. It sat in front of them and whined. Blood stained its neck.

"She's hurt," Zoe said, kneeling to carefully pet her.

But Riley's concern wasn't for the dog. "Give me your flashlight."

Zoe stood, obviously alarmed at her tone. "What's wrong?"

Riley took the flashlight and scanned the tree line, eyes peeled.

"Wait, how do you know the dog?" Zoe asked.

Riley began backing away. "We need to get inside."

"Riley?"

"She belongs to the hunter."

Zoe's face fell. "You mean he's here?"

"He must be."

"What about her? We can't leave her. She's hurt."

"Let's go. If she follows us she can come with. If not, then I assume she's waiting for her master. And that's something I don't want to be caught doing."

They hurried back toward the cabin as best they could in the deep snow. The dog did its best to keep up. When they reached the back door, Riley unlocked it and allowed both Zoe and the dog entry. Then she bolted the door and stood by it for a while, watching intently as the snow danced in front of her in the black night.

"She's cut," Zoe said from in front of the fireplace. "On her chest."

Riley turned to look at them. The dog was licking Zoe's hand as she petted her.

"She's sweet too," Zoe said.

"Yeah, I just wonder where her master is."

"Do you have a first aid kit?"

Riley turned back to the window. "Under the sink."

Zoe went to fetch it and the dog followed. Soon they were back in front of the firelight. "Can you come hold the flashlight while I tend to her wound?"

Riley slid out of her coat and slid the gun into her waistband. She held the flashlight as Zoe first cleaned, then bandaged the dog.

"She smells like gasoline," Zoe said, looking up at Riley.

Riley stared back at the black windows. "Yeah, I noticed that too." She placed her hand on the gun and wondered if the dog had had a hand in helping mess with their generator. "I don't think anyone will be getting any sleep tonight."

CHAPTER THIRTY-TWO

Zoe awoke to bright white light streaming through the windows. It took her several moments for her to remember where she was and what all had happened. When she did recall, she sat up from her slumber on the couch, and allowed her blankets to fall to her feet. Next to her, Riley slept with her feet on the floor, head back on the cushion. She had her hand resting on the gun in her waistband. At the fireplace, the logs smoldered, while the dog they'd found lounged in front of it. As Zoe stirred some more, the dog rose and came to her, tail wagging slowly.

"Hello, girl." She licked Zoe's hand.

Riley's eyes flickered open, and the dog ran to the door and scratched.

Zoe rose to let her out.

"Hi," she said on her way to the door.

"Hi."

Riley stood and stretched. "Anything weird happen while we were asleep?"

"Nothing that I'm aware of."

"How's the dog?"

"I think she's okay. She just went out to do her business."

But the dog reappeared at the door and looked at Zoe and yipped. Zoe opened the door for her, but she just stood there barking up at her.

"She wants us to go with," Riley said. "Just as well. I want to know what made that awful noise last night."

"What about the hunter?"

"He hasn't come yet, so I'm not worried about him coming now. Besides, I have the gun. You can stay if you want."

"No way."

Zoe stepped into her boots and shrugged into her coat. Then the three of them were off, down the patio steps and back out toward the trail.

"Sun's out," Riley said as they trudged through the snow. "Maybe we'll get that melt."

"Hope so."

Suddenly, the dog took off ahead and Riley cocked the trigger on her gun.

"You think he's here?" Zoe said, ready to flee at any given second.

"Could be, why else would she take off like that?"

They followed the dog slowly down the trail, eyes and gun trained ahead. The dog was about fifty yards ahead of them when she went off trail and down the wooded embankment.

"Look," Riley said, pointing down at the snow. "Tire tracks."

"Oh my God." Zoe's heart leapt to her throat.

"They run off the road up ahead."

They both ran as best they could, following the tire marks. When they reached the edge of the embankment, Zoe noticed the swath of small trees that had been standing were now flattened all the way to the bottom, about two hundred yards below.

And there, at the bottom, was a dark blue SUV on its top, tires pointed up at the sky.

They inched closer. Zoe gasped as she saw the dog reach its destination. A man was lying close to the vehicle, body contorted in a way that strongly suggested he wasn't alive.

"That's him," Riley said. "That's the hunter."

Zoe covered her mouth and turned, unable to watch the dog paw at her lifeless master.

"Looks like it."

Riley rubbed her forehead. "Well, I guess we don't have to worry about him anymore."

Zoe knew she should be relieved, but she wasn't. Maybe it was too soon to relax. Maybe in a couple of hours it would settle in.

"Zoe, look," Riley said, reaching for her hand to ease her back toward the embankment. She pointed. "Over there, caught in those trees. Isn't that your—"

"My tent." Her voice shook. Son of a bitch.

She turned away again. Unwilling to see what else the man had had with him that had been strewn from his vehicle as it rolled down the mountainside.

Riley came to her side and wrapped an arm around her. "It's okay. It's all okay now."

"Then why don't I feel better?"

"Just give it time," she said, tugging her closer. She turned and whistled for the dog. A few moments later, the dog joined them near the back patio.

Zoe leaned against Riley, needing her support now more than ever. "I can't believe it's over," she said. "I just can't believe it."

They reached the door and Riley tilted her chin. "Hey, believe it, okay? You survived. We survived. It's all over." She smiled at her. "Why don't you go give our new friend a bath to make her feel more at home while I try to call the sheriff?"

A chill ran through her again as she thought of the dead hunter. The man who'd been hunting her. But the dog pressed against her, wanting her attention, so she chose to focus on her.

"She does smell pretty bad, doesn't she?"

Riley nodded.

"Hey, why do I have to do it?"

"Because caring for her will take your mind off things. Unless you want to be the one to call the sheriff?"

"Uh, no, you go right ahead." She knew she was doomed in having to face a million questions. But for now, Riley was right. She needed to keep her mind on other things.

So for the first time in over a year, her thoughts went to something other than her stalker.

CHAPTER THIRTY-THREE

Riley smiled as she made her way to the kitchen in the low candlelight and heard Zoe in the bathroom with the dog. She was talking to her softly, encouraging her to let her bathe her as best she could with heated water from the fireplace. Soon the bathroom opened, and the dog came running out and promptly headed for the fireplace, where she relaxed and began licking her paws.

Riley removed the gun from her waist band and set it back in the curio on the top shelf, glad to be rid of it. She hadn't said as much, but Zoe too, now seemed more content, as if a weight had been lifted off both their shoulders.

Riley turned as Zoe emerged from the bathroom. Her hair was wet and she was dressed in sleep pants and a sweatshirt.

"You're all clean, too?" Riley asked.

"Yep. Only I had to bathe in the cold water. The dog got all the nice, hot water."

Riley chuckled. "Well, you both smell fabulous."

"Did you get a hold of the sheriff?"

"Nah, but I finally got a text through to Keira. She and Elise are coming up as soon as they can. They're also notifying the sheriff for us. So, it may be a long night once the sheriff's department arrives."

They walked into the living room where Riley headed for the fireplace to rekindle the fire. But Zoe stopped her by tugging on her hand, pulling her down onto the couch.

"Don't mess with the fire," she said softly.

"Why not? You'll get cold."

"Huh-uh. I don't think so." She inched closer to Riley, snuggling tight and pulling the blanket down over them. "Besides, I like the low light of the candle. It's romantic."

Riley eyed the glowing candle on the coffee table. With the overcast sky, the room was only alive with its ambient light. Zoe was right, it was a bit romantic. She could always tend to the fire later.

Zoe inched ever closer. "Mm, smells like someone else cleaned up a little as well."

"I did."

"Well, you smell fabulous too." She laughed softly and nuzzled her neck.

Riley felt her body come alive in gooseflesh. She had to grip her own knee in order not to react.

"Are you intentionally trying to turn me on?" Riley asked.

"I don't know. Maybe. Is it working?"

"Yes," Riley breathed. "So you better slow down."

"Slow down?" Zoe said, sounding like she had absolutely no intention of doing anything of the sort. "Whatever for?"

"Zoe," Riley whispered. But the next thing she knew, Zoe was straddling her, eyes alive and fierce.

"What? We have some time before they arrive. Don't we?"

Riley placed her hands on her hips. "Yes, I'm assuming with the roads like they are. But—this is—are you—?"

"Sure? Yes, more than I've ever been."

"I mean are you sure this isn't just your reaction to all of this being over?"

"So what if it is? I feel free for the first time in months and along the way I met this wonderful, incredible person, who is literally sitting here in my arms, looking at me in a way that no one else has ever looked at me before. So, what's wrong with my wanting to capture that? Grab hold of it and make it mine?"

Riley didn't speak. Couldn't speak. She was lost in her eyes and the conviction of her words.

"Nothing," she managed.

Zoe held her face and searched her eyes. Then she kissed her. Soft and slow, tentative and controlled. As if she were tasting something decadent for the very first time and she wanted to memorize how it tasted and felt all at once.

Riley's head swam in liquid bliss, hot and languid, like she was awash in ecstasy. She thought about gripping her harder, about flipping her and pinning her down to the couch and ravishing her, but she was too caught up in the slow motion of it all. Too captivated by the mystery and the seeking, the learning of one another.

"Riley," Zoe panted when she finally drew away. "Is it always this good?"

"No," Riley said, delirious. "This is all you."

Zoe pressed tighter into her, trying to grind herself against Riley's stomach, as if she were desperate for contact. Riley gave her what she wanted and pressed her hand against her crotch. Zoe sighed and kissed her harder. Plunged her tongue into her mouth and took her with a vengeance. Riley leaned back, helpless, and allowed her to consume her, thoroughly enjoying every second.

Then Zoe stopped, tore her mouth away from her, and stood.

"What's wrong?"

She grinned. "Absolutely nothing." She pulled off her sweatshirt, revealing a thin T-shirt beneath it. She removed that as well and tossed it to Riley, who caught it in midair.

Zoe stood before her topless, small, taut breasts puckered in the chilly air, her body glowing in the firelight.

Riley was breathless, trying to keep up with what was happening. She nearly lost her mind when Zoe began running her hands over her body seductively, down to the sleep pants, where she slowly and deliberately removed them along with her underwear.

"Jesus," Riley said. "You're magnificent."

Zoe walked slowly toward her, like a cat closing in on prey. When she reached her she straddled her again and held her face.

"Make me feel good, Riley," she whispered. "Please."

She started grinding again and Riley found her wet center and slid her hand into her hot, slick folds. Zoe sighed again and threw her head back, arching her body. Riley took advantage and leaned forward and enveloped her breast with her mouth, causing Zoe to cry out and clutch her head.

"Riley," she panted. "Oh, God." She quickened her hips and plunged her tongue deep into Riley's mouth. She rode her hand hard, moaning and groaning. Soon, she'd pulled away for air, body undulating, eyes trained on the ceiling, her flawless skin reflecting the candlelight.

"Riley," she cried. "Riley."

"Yes, Zoe. Come for me, baby."

Zoe clenched her eyes and bucked three times wildly and then threw her eyes open, reared her head back, and screamed.

"Oh, my God," Riley whispered, watching in awe. "Jesus, you are so goddamned fucking beautiful."

Zoe gripped her wrist and took all she could from her, body tight and taut, moving in what Riley knew to be involuntary motions. The dance of her was mesmerizing, hypnotic, addicting. And Riley knew she could be a voyeur of Zoe's for all eternity.

Zoe laughed as she came down, her eyelids heavy with satiation, her mouth a tilted grin. She leaned down and kissed Riley softly, slowly.

"Feel good?" Riley asked, talking softly in her ear.

"Mm-hm. But…"

"But?"

She touched Riley's lips with a tender finger. "I want more."

Riley smiled.

"I want you inside me. Can you…do that?"

"Oh, yes, I can do that."

"Will you, please?"

Riley gently slid her hand along her wet folds, using her excitement as lubrication. Then she carefully inserted two fingers into her and watched in amazement as Zoe reacted.

Her eyes widened and narrowed and a quick, sharp breath escaped her. Then she began to move. Slowly at first, hips performing a slow, sensual dance as her eyes grew heavy and then rolled back in her head.

"Oh, Riley," she rasped. "Riley, fuck. Mm, yes."

"Feel me, baby. Feel me inside you." Riley moved her fingers up deep inside and Zoe gasped and squeezed her eyes closed.

"Ah! Mm, yes."

Then Riley pressed against her G-spot and Zoe lost her mind. She cried out and opened her eyes and pinned Riley to the spot with her hungry stare.

"Yes, Riley. Just like that. Please. Oh, God it's good. It's so good."

She thrust her hips wildly and held fast to Riley's shoulders.

"Riley. God. Yes."

"Ride me, baby," Riley said. "Fucking ride me as hard as you want."

Zoe groaned and kissed her ravenously, sucking and tugging on her lips. Riley was so fucking turned on she started to move herself, trying to grind herself against the couch.

"Riley!" Zoe called. "Riley." She jerked faster, bucked harder. "More! More now!"

Riley fucked her good and hard then and she came in an explosion of screams and wetness, riding Riley's hand, saturating her fingers. She rode her until her body appeared it could take no more and she collapsed atop her, desperate for breath, but laughing in her ear.

"Dear God," she said. She drew back and stared down at an awe inspired Riley. "That was fucking incredible."

"You're telling me."

"You did all that with your fingers?"

"Uh-huh." Riley raised an eyebrow. "You surprised?"

"Um, yeah. I had no idea."

"Seriously?"

"Seriously."

"Well, wait until you see what I can do with my mouth."

Zoe laughed and shoved her back, forcing her against the cushions.

"My God, you just made me want it again."

"That surprise you too?"

"Yes." She bent down and kissed her. Softly, tentatively. "Everything about my time with you has surprised me."

Riley kissed her back, lost in the taste of her. "Good, because I've got so much more to show you."

CHAPTER THIRTY-FOUR

The sheriff's department knocked on the door at dawn, startling Zoe out of a deep sleep wrapped in Riley's arms. They dressed quickly and headed downstairs. Two deputies stood waiting at the back door, their breath coming out in plumes of white mist. One kept shifting his feet and blowing into his gloved hands.

"You Riley Robinson?" the tall one asked as Riley opened the door. The dog barked but Zoe quickly calmed her.

"I am."

"I'm Deputy Burgess and this is Deputy Hyde. Mind if we come in?"

Zoe's stomach lurched as she heard voices and motors off in the distance. Overhead, a helicopter approached.

Riley pushed open the door and allowed the officers entry. She introduced Zoe and led them into the living room.

"Sorry we don't have any power," Riley said, moving to sit on the adjacent chair from the couch where the deputies settled. "Guess there's a line down somewhere or something."

Zoe approached nervously, wringing her fingers. Riley motioned for her to come closer, and Zoe rested on the armrest of the chair. Riley held her hand.

"No, not that we're aware of," Deputy Burgess said, looking at them curiously.

Zoe clenched Riley's hand, the deputy pretty much confirming what she'd feared. Someone had messed with their power.

"You want to tell us what happened?" Burgess continued.

"About the accident?" Riley asked.

"Please."

Riley cleared her throat with obvious nerves. "Night before last we heard a crashing sound. A terrible crashing sound."

"Like something huge was rolling down the mountain," Zoe said.

"We had no idea what is was."

"And that's when you went out and found the deceased?" Burgess asked.

"No. Not that night. We went out but it was pitch-black. We couldn't see anything. We found the dog. Or more like she found us. We got scared and came back inside."

"When did you find the deceased?"

"The following morning. We saw the tire tracks in the snow. Saw where he went off the edge."

"Did you call for help?"

"Tried to. Couldn't get through. And well, he was obviously dead."

"But she managed to reach her friend," Zoe said.

"Yes, and they called you."

The shorter deputy, Deputy Hyde, looked up from his small notepad. "Did you have any contact with the deceased?"

"Uh, yes," Riley said. "I met him once a few days ago and then we saw him again the day of the accident."

"Anything unusual happen during those meetings?"

Riley looked to Zoe. She squeezed her hand. Zoe swallowed and nodded.

"I think he's the man who's been stalking me," Zoe said.

Both deputies looked at her. "Someone's been stalking you?"

"Yes, and we believe it was this…man," Riley said.

"It's a long story," Zoe said.

Deputy Burgess stood as a female deputy knocked on the door. Zoe quickly shushed the dog. She could feel her own face flushed with nerves. She wondered briefly if she was as bright red as she felt.

The deputies spoke at the door. Then the female left. Burgess turned to them. He looked at Zoe and Hyde stood as if he knew what he was going to say.

"Ma'am. Why don't you stay here with me and fill me in on your stalker theory and Ms. Robinson can go with Deputy Hyde."

"It's not a theory," Zoe said. She looked to Riley and Riley held up her hand as if to tell her to keep her cool. She stood and kissed her forehead and then shrugged into her coat and stepped into her boots. She left with Deputy Hyde and the dog whined and came to Zoe's side as if she could sense her qualms.

"Why don't we start at the beginning," Burgess said, making himself comfortable. Zoe wiped a tear, already fearing that he would doubt her story. But she steeled herself, stroked the dog, and began. From the beginning.

Chapter Thirty-five

Riley walked with Hyde back to the road where a small swarm of sheriff vehicles were gathered. Overhead, the helicopter was hovering and blowing icy shards of snow off the trees. Riley held her hand protectively to her face as they approached the edge where the SUV had run off course.

Deputy Hyde glanced down at the scene below and then spoke loudly.

"So, you didn't know the deceased then?"

Riley shook her head. "No, I didn't know him, and Zoe said she didn't recognize him. Though she couldn't really get a good look at him. He was always wearing a hat and stayed a short distance away."

Hyde nodded. They both watched as the rescue personnel on the ground began strapping the lifeless body into a metal rescue stretcher attached to the helicopter. One of the men gave a signal and the helicopter rose, hoisting the body up with it. Riley craned her head to watch, and the helicopter flew high overhead and down the road to where an ambulance was waiting. More rescue personnel hovered nearby as the body was lowered to the ground. The team released the stretcher from the helicopter, allowing the chopper to fly away.

Riley lowered her hand, the wisping snow now dying down.

Deputy Hyde flipped through his notes and spoke. "Deceased was one Harold Donald Dyson out of Scottsdale. That name mean anything to you?"

"No."

"But you're reasonably sure he was stalking your friend?"

"Yes."

"What makes you think that?"

"The stuff she's told me and the fact that his presence here was odd."

"How's that?"

"He came up to hunt in the middle of a snowstorm. And he said he was hunting turkey. It's too late in the season to hunt turkey. And then we had the power outage. I think someone's messed with my generator and my Bronco. Neither work and there's evidence they've been tampered with."

"And you think it was Mr. Dyson?"

"Well, yeah. He's the only one we've seen and he, I don't know, acted strangely. Asked strange questions."

"Such as?"

"He asked if we knew of anyone staying in the abandoned cabin up the way. Well, that's Zoe's grandfather's cabin and she, up until a little over a week ago, was staying in it."

"And how's that strange?"

"Because the whole reason she was up here staying in it was to hide from whoever is stalking her. He just made it sound like he knew who she was, like he'd found her and was rubbing it in. Toying with her. It really creeped us out."

Up ahead, the rescue team loaded the body into the ambulance and headed down the mountain, emergency lights off. A group of sheriff's personnel stood talking together, while down below more members examined the truck and took photos of the scene.

In her mind, Riley could still see the mangled body of Mr. Dyson and it chilled her to the core.

"And how long have you known Zoe?" Hyde asked.

Riley swallowed and squinted toward the pale sun. "A little over a week."

He blinked at her. But he didn't comment. He just made notes in his little pad. "And how did you come to know her?"

"We met down at the Safeway. We were both buying supplies for our stay up here on the mountain. Then we ran into each other up here and I noticed she was staying in that ramshackle cabin with no heat, so I invited her to stay with me in my cabin."

"You invited a stranger into your cabin?"

"Yes, I did. And I'd do it again. She was freezing."

"And she said she was hiding from a stalker?"

"Yes."

"And you believe her?"

"Yes, I do." Riley steeled her jaw. Hyde just kept making notes.

"So you don't know her background, whether or not she's on any medication of any kind? Whether she's mentally stable—"

"She's not crazy, if that's what you're getting at."

Hyde cleared his throat and she almost dared him to say something more about Zoe's mental health. He wisely chose not to.

"You're the owner of this cabin?"

"Yes. I've had it about nine months."

"But your main residence is where?"

"Phoenix."

"Do you plan on staying here for a while, or are you heading back home?"

"I'm not sure, but I'll definitely be here through the weekend."

He scratched his brow. "Make sure you are as we may have more questions. If you choose to go home, let us know first."

She nodded.

"That's all for now."

"Okay." She shoved her hands in her coat pockets and stared down at the wreckage. The deputy didn't sound like he was totally convinced of her story, and she wondered how Zoe was fairing with Burgess. She sighed and squinted toward the sun again. She should've been appreciative that the storm was now over, that Mr. Dyson was dead. She should've appreciated how the sun felt shining on her face. But none of that seemed to comfort her.

Because, for whatever reason, this whole thing felt far from over.

Chapter Thirty-six

Zoe straightened and wiped her eyes as Riley walked in the door. Deputy Burgess had just left, and she couldn't be more relieved. The man had questioned her for over an hour, and she got the strong sense that he didn't believe a word she said. Her bursting into tears when he'd asked if she was on any medication certainly didn't help matters any.

"Hey," Riley said, coming to her side and sitting. "It was that bad, eh?"

Riley continued to wipe her face, committed to hide her tears and put on a brave face. "Somewhat," she said. "I don't think he believes me about the stalker though."

"Well, fuck him, then. He'll find out all he needs to know when they look into Mr. Dyson's background. Then he'll change his tune."

"Dyson," Zoe said shaking her name. "It just doesn't sound familiar to me at all. I don't get it. Why did he choose me?"

"I don't know. Did Burgess tell you anything about him?"

"No. Just his name."

"They probably don't know a whole lot at this point."

Zoe sniffled. "Probably not." She looked at Riley. "Did they act like you were crazy when you told them we've only known each other a week?"

Riley laughed. "A little, yeah." She touched her face. "But I don't care, do you? We don't owe them an explanation for how we feel."

"No, I suppose not. I'm just so tired of everyone acting like I'm crazy."

"Hey, I believe you. Okay? And I gotta count for something."

Zoe smiled and leaned into her soft hand. "You do."

Riley scooted closer and kissed her forehead. Then her lips. "Mm, you taste good. Salty."

Zoe laughed.

Riley ran her thumbs across her cheeks. "Don't cry, love. It'll be over soon. And then you can move on, free as a bird."

"I hope so."

"I know so."

Riley opened her arms and Zoe snuggled into her and stared into the fire. "The worst thing about all this is how helpless I feel. How weak."

"But you're not," Riley said. "You've fought back, taken matters into your own hands. Changed the game. That takes guts. A lot of guts."

"Look at where it got me, though. Freezing to death in a run-down cabin. A lunatic chasing me on a mountain during a snowstorm."

"It got you me. And pretty girl over there."

Zoe looked at the dog who was sound asleep by the fire.

"I think we're pretty good prizes, aren't we?"

Zoe smiled and kissed her hand. "Yes, the best, actually." She cocked her head. "I wonder if we'll have to give her back. Like if Dyson had a family or something."

"Don't worry about that. Besides, a guy like him, I doubt he was married. How would he have the time to run around and chase you if he was?"

"True."

Riley pulled her closer. "Just relax and enjoy the peace. You deserve it."

Zoe snuggled closer, loving the way she felt against her. "You know what, I think you're right."

Riley chuckled. "I usually am."

CHAPTER THIRTY-SEVEN

R iley stood in the near dark of dusk using a flashlight to look at the cut wires to the house.

"Goddammit. Zoe was right." *Why didn't I check? Why didn't I come out here and check?*

Because you didn't believe her then.

"Damn it!"

She kicked at the snow and then walked over to the breaker box, opened it, saw that all the breakers had been turned off, and then slammed the door closed.

"Motherfucker switched off the breakers, then cut the power lines."

She stalked back to the house, upset at herself for not checking the night Zoe suggested it might've been done purposely, and upset at herself for not checking when the sheriff's department was there. Because that right there was proof alone, that what Zoe was saying was true.

Dyson had cut their power. And probably screwed with the generator.

She stomped the snow off her feet and stepped inside. The house smelled of stew, and Zoe was sitting and cooking with a pot over the flames.

"What's wrong?" she asked the second she saw Riley.

"Well, you were right. We didn't lose power because of the storm. It was the hunter, Dyson, and there's no way I can fix it." She took off her coat and boots and sank down onto the sofa with her cell phone in hand.

"How do you know?" Zoe asked.

"I just saw where he cut the lines." She located the number to the power company as Zoe sat staring in silence. To her surprise and relief, she got through. She reported her situation quickly, still afraid she'd lose the connection. She didn't, but that was the end of the good news. The customer service rep told her they couldn't get someone out to fix it for a few days. The storm had them backed up with calls.

Riley thanked the woman and ended the call. "Looks like we're gonna be roughing it for a few more days."

Zoe shrugged as she stirred. "I don't know. Doesn't bother me much. I kind of like it."

"Those cold showers growing on you?"

"No. I heat my water. You're the one who's insisting on the cold showers."

"Yeah, well, after today, I'm changing my mind. I'm ready for some power and some heat. I've had enough of roughing it."

Zoe began ladling the stew into bowls. "I thought you liked the cold because it meant we could snuggle."

"I'm all for cuddling. But imagine doing it, not because we're freezing, but because we want to." She wriggled her eyebrows and Zoe laughed.

"Okay, yeah you got me. That does sound nice. But in the meantime I'll just enjoy us making our own heat."

"Mm," Riley said as she joined her by the fire. "You got that right."

She took her offered bowl and leaned in to give Zoe a lingering kiss. "If this didn't smell so damn good, I'd say we should go get busy making our own heat right now."

"And I'd agree with you." She kissed her back and then they both settled in to eat. Outside, darkness fell and once they finished with their meal, they lounged by the fire in each other's arms, with Zoe resting back into Riley.

"You're beautiful in the firelight," Riley said into her ear.

"So are you."

"You wanna go make out on the couch?"

"Mm, what's wrong with right here?"

She turned in Riley's arms and stroked her face. Then she smiled and kissed her and it was as wonderful and as hot as the fire.

"God, you're a good kisser," Riley said.

"You too. I love how you go slow and take your time with me."

"I was thinking the same thing about you."

They kissed some more, both taking their time and teasing, drawing out the sensual pleasure of tasting one another.

But just as Zoe made a noise of pure bliss, the dog jumped up and barked and ran to the back window.

Zoe jerked and drew away and Riley turned to look out into the darkness.

"What's she barking at?" Zoe asked, sounding afraid.

Riley stood and joined the dog by the back door. She unlocked it and opened it and stuck her head outside. The night was already black, the stars like tiny shining diamonds in the sky. She inhaled the crisp air and glanced around, once then twice. The dog edged beyond her legs and took off across the patio, sliding near the rails, barking wildly.

"What is it?" Zoe asked, peeking out from behind her.

"Nothing, I don't see a thing."

The dog pawed at the rails and then moved like she was going to run down the stairs and give chase.

"No, no, no," Riley said, catching her. She grabbed her by the collar and encouraged her to walk back inside the house. "I don't want you taking off in this weather. You'd end up a puppysicle."

They came back inside and Zoe pushed on the door to close and lock it. She hugged herself from the chill that had infiltrated the living room.

"What do you think she was barking at?"

"I don't know. Probably elk. They like to walk around about dusk."

"But it's dark now."

"Maybe there's a straggler or two. Who knows? Dogs are silly."

Riley settled the dog back by the fire and then came to Zoe who looked frightened like she had the very first night she'd stayed with her.

"Zoe, don't. I'm sure it's nothing. The bad guy's gone, remember? Nothing to worry about."

"I know, it's just déjà vu I guess."

"Well, here's what I think of your déjà vu." Riley tugged her in close and kissed her. Deeply.

Zoe pulled away, breathless. "Wow, maybe I should have déjà vu more often."

Riley laughed and picked her up and Zoe wrapped her legs around her.

"You taking me somewhere, Ms. Robinson?"

"You bet I am."

"And where would that be?"

Riley headed for the staircase to her bedroom. "Someplace where we can create our own heat.

Zoe laughed and nibbled her neck.

"In that case, you better hurry. I'm getting hot already."

Chapter Thirty-eight

Zoe awoke to soft kisses along her spine. She sighed as they moved upward and warm hands smoothed over her skin to her breasts where they awakened and teased her nipples. She groaned when hungry fingers framed and lightly squeezed them, pulling the pleasure up and out of the tips.

"Mm, good morning," Riley said, kissing her neck and nuzzling her ear.

"I'll say," Zoe whispered, already turning over to offer more of her body.

"How did you sleep?" Riley asked as she continued her kisses along the column of her neck while her hand still played the ache in her breast.

"Not well."

"I know, the dog must really be into those elk or whatever critter was out there."

Her mouth found Zoe's bunched nipple and Zoe cried out and knotted her hair in her hands.

"She kept—interrupting us," Zoe breathed.

"Well, it's daylight now. So let's see if we can have a little fun."

She flicked her nipple with her tongue and Zoe gasped in surprise. Riley knew just what to do to send her over the edge into madness. And she seemed to thoroughly enjoy doing it.

"What kind of fun would you like this morning, madam?" Riley asked as she continued to tease her with her hot mouth.

"Um—agh—I don't know." She could hardly form words Riley was driving her so insane.

"You don't know?"

"No."

"Well, does it feel good?"

"Ye—es. Really good."

"And you like it?"

"Uh-huh."

"Well, would you like it somewhere else?"

Zoe opened her eyes. She pressed her lips together. Quickly, she nodded her head.

Riley laughed wickedly. "Say it."

"Huh-uh."

"Come on, tell me. Tell me what you want."

"Riley."

"Come on. Own it. You can do it."

Zoe palmed her forehead, her face already heating. "I want you to do to me what you did the other night by the fire."

"Which was…"

"Riley."

"Come on."

Zoe blushed even harder. She'd never had a lover like Riley before. One who had awakened her entire body in several different ways. And she wasn't used to asking for what she wanted.

Riley however, seemed to get turned on by her doing just that.

"I want you to—you know—kiss me—down there."

"Down where?"

Zoe rolled her eyes. "You know where."

Riley feigned innocence. "No, I don't think I do. You better tell me."

Zoe sighed, frustrated, and Riley countered by teasing her nipples some more, this time using the slightest pressure from her teeth.

"Okay, okay," Zoe said, arching up into her.

"I want you to kiss me between my legs."

"Where?"

"Here." Zoe spread her legs and placed her hand on her center.

"Here?" Riley asked as she traced her hand down to Zoe's.

"Yes. Please."

Riley grinned and came back up and kissed her mouth. "We're going to have to work on your assertiveness." Then she trailed back down her body with soft kisses and lingered around her thighs.

"God, I can feel your heat," she said from between her legs. "And you're so wet you're glistening."

Riley breathed on her aching flesh, teasing her more. Zoe arched into her and grabbed her head.

"Riley, please."

"Please, what?"

"Make me feel good."

"With pleasure," Riley said. And she lowered her mouth and licked Zoe's flesh, first playfully, little flicks here and there, toying with her clit. And then when she had Zoe thrashing and begging, she dove in and licked her full on hard, up and down, over and over, sending Zoe into outer space.

Zoe cried out again and again, grabbing fistfuls of her hair, begging and pleading. She'd never felt such intense pleasure. Given completely and then taken away. Over and over again. At last, she lost all control and she came up off the bed and demanded Riley do as she wanted.

"Riley, goddammit, make me come. Make me come so hard."

Riley didn't waste a second. She enveloped her in her mouth and made love to her clit with her tongue and powerful tugs of her mouth. Zoe thrashed and groaned, called out to God above and demanded Riley perform harder and faster, until she was bucking her hips up into her face and holding her head tightly in her hands, fucking her with all her might.

And then she came. And the room around her drew in all at once and then exploded along with her body into a million little shattered pieces, falling like confetti all around. She came and she came and she came. Riley feeding from her like a mad woman, more confetti shooting up and then falling down, sprinkling down like gently falling snow, until she was so spent and so exhausted that she fell limp against the bed, her breath rough and ragged in her chest, Riley still gripped in her hands.

And just as she was enjoying her bliss, the dog barked again and Zoe jerked and sat up, Riley right there with her.

"What the fuck is wrong with that dog?"

Then there was knocking. And a little voice carrying through the glass.

"Riley Robinson, I'm here!"

CHAPTER THIRTY-NINE

Oh, I hope we didn't disturb anything," Elise said as they walked in. Riley tightened her bathrobe and gave an uncomfortable looking smile while Zoe moved about trying to straighten the living room. She, at least, had gotten dressed. Riley, on the other hand, had bolted down the stairs as quickly as she could to answer the door.

"No, no," Riley blurted, still smiling. "Didn't interrupt anything."

Keira gave her a look. "Uh-huh."

Phoenix ran for the dog and Elise stopped him, scooping him up quickly. "Not yet, honey. We don't know anything about the dog."

"She's okay," Zoe said.

"Who's is she?" Elise asked.

"She was the...man's. We found her after the accident."

"Oh."

"Can I pet her, Mama? Please?"

Elise sat with Phoenix on her lap and the dog ran right up to them and licked his hands. Phoenix laughed and Elise showed him how to pet her.

"She belongs to him?" Keira asked softly as Riley closed the door.

Zoe joined Riley on the chair while Keira joined her family on the couch.

"She did, yes," Riley said.

Keira shook her head. "Man, you'll have to fill me in on everything. Sounds crazy."

"It was," Zoe said softly. She ran her hand through her hair wondering if Keira and Elise would judge her and disbelieve her like everyone else had.

Phoenix giggled again at the dog and then looked up at Elise. "Mama, it's cold in here."

Riley stood and hurried to the fireplace. "Sorry, bud, but it may be cold for a while. We'll make lots of s'mores though, okay?"

"Actually, I think we'll be fine," Keira said with a smile.

"Tell her, babe."

"We brought you a new generator."

"What?" Riley looked shocked.

"We did. It's out in the SUV."

"But—"

Elise held up her hand to stop her. "We figured it was the least we could do since you're going to be letting us use the cabin."

"Well, of course, you guys are always welcome, but you didn't have to do that."

"Well, we did. And you can't refuse it. Especially now that it's needed."

Riley blinked. Then looked to Zoe in disbelief. Zoe smiled at her.

"It's very generous," Zoe said. "Like you."

"Exactly," Keira said. "So no arguing over it. Go get dressed and help me unload it."

Riley hurried up the stairs and Phoenix got down off his mother to come say hello to Zoe. He placed his little hands on her legs and looked at her with his big blue eyes.

"I'm glad you're still here," he said. "You make it funner."

Zoe laughed. "I do? Well, that's nice to hear."

"Will you be here all the days that I am?"

"I'm not sure."

"We're only staying the weekend again. We have work. What do you do, Zoe?" Elise asked.

"I'm an ultrasound technician."

"Oh, wow. That must be very interesting," Keira said.

"It is."

"So, you like it then?"

"Yes, very much."

"Are you taking some vacation time, then?"

She shifted, growing uncomfortable. "Not exactly." It was true. In fact, she wondered if she'd have a job to return to. The last they knew she was out sick.

"Oh," Elise said.

"Hey, Zoe," Phoenix said, playing with her leather bracelet. "Will you come look for Bigfoot with me?"

"Sure. If that's okay with your mothers."

Keira shrugged. "Fine by me."

"Don't go far," Elise said.

Phoenix was already bouncing up and down. "Come on, come on, let's go. Can we bring the dog, too?"

"Sure."

Zoe and Phoenix put on their coats and stepped outside with the dog. The day was sunny and warmer than it had been, with the snow and ice beginning to melt from the patio and the treetops. Zoe was glad to be out of the house and out from under Elise's eyes. She always seemed to ask the most difficult questions. Granted, they probably wouldn't be difficult for someone living under normal circumstances, but her life, lately, had been anything but normal. And Elise was someone who homed in on that and wanted to know more. She hoped Riley would do most of the filling in and she hoped it would all sound better coming from Riley.

In the meantime, she'd hang out with Phoenix. A good nature walk was just what she needed. And the dog, it seemed, was very much enjoying herself as well. Hurrying from tree to tree, nose to the ground, tail wagging.

"What's her name?" Phoenix asked.

"The dog? I don't know. She didn't have a name tag."

"She has to have a name, Phoenix said. "Everybody gots a name."

"Well, how about we name her, then? Huh? What do you say?"

"Yeah!"

"Great, okay, you pick."

He skipped along ahead of her as they went back into the pines, the dog walking ahead of him.

"Um, Princess," he said.

Zoe laughed. "I don't know if she'd like that. I mean, can you picture her dressed up like a princess?"

"No, not really. I know *I* wouldn't want to dress up like a princess."

"Me neither," Zoe said.

"What about Peanut Butter? Or Snowflake?" he said and then shook his head. He stopped and dropped his hands down by his side in obvious frustration. "I don't know, Zoe. I don't got many ideas."

"Hmm, how about Shiloh?"

"Shiloh," he said as if trying the word on in his mouth. "Yeah! I like it."

"Okay, then, Shiloh it is."

"Here, Shiloh, here girl," Phoenix called out as he chased after her.

They continued walking peacefully until a cracking sound sent Shiloh taking off at warp speed, sprinting and barking.

Phoenix gave chase and Zoe took off as well, chasing him. But she tripped on a tree root and fell hard, face-first, eating the ground. She lay still for a moment, trying to get her bearings. The earth smelled moist and fresh and she could hear Phoenix calling out for Shiloh in the distance. Realizing he was getting farther and farther away, she pushed herself up with a groan and hurried after him. But just a few yards in, she realized she'd lost him.

Chapter Forty

I don't understand what happened," Elise said, wiping Phoenix's face with a washcloth. The dirt was coming off, but he was still shedding tears.

"It was Bigfoot, Mama," he cried.

"Oh, honey, shh, it's okay." Elise pulled him in tight for a hug and gave Zoe an angry look. "I mean, how could you lose him?"

"I'm sorry, I fell. I was running after him when I got tripped up. And by the time I got back up, he was out of sight." She winced as Riley cleaned her up as best she could with a warm washcloth. She wiped her brow and held the washcloth to her bloody lip. Then she set in on her skinned hands.

"Thank God he came back," Keira said, pacing the floor by the fire. "You couldn't see him at all?"

"No, I—couldn't. I could hear Shiloh—"

"Who's Shiloh?" Keira asked, confused.

"The dog, Mama. We named her."

"Right. Go on."

"I could hear Shiloh and Phoenix calling after her and then they just went silent. I kept running but couldn't see them. Then, after calling and calling for them, I heard Shiloh give a vicious bark and suddenly there was Phoenix, sprinting back toward me, Shiloh on his heels."

"And you didn't see anyone else?" Riley asked.

"No."

"It was Bigfoot!" Phoenix yelled. He started crying again, obviously upset that no one was listening to him.

"Okay, love, shhh." Elise held him and rocked him. "Tell Mamas what you saw."

He took in some shaky breaths and wiped his eyes with his fists. "Bigfoot, I told you."

"Well, what did Bigfoot look like?" Keira asked.

"He was big and white and had lots of fur up here." He touched his head and cheeks. "And he grabbed me and told me to be quiet."

"What?" Keira asked, alarmed.

"He did this." Phoenix put his finger to his mouth. "And he grabbed me real hard on my arm."

Elise looked at his arm and rubbed it. "I don't see anything," she said to Keira.

"He did!" Phoenix said.

"Okay, little man, we believe you," Keira said, crossing to give him a kiss. "Why don't you and Mama go lie down for a little while, okay?"

"'K." He rubbed his eyes again. "Can Shiloh come?"

"Sure, love, Shiloh can come."

The three of them headed for the bedroom and Keira sank down on the couch. "Well, he sure thinks he saw something," she said.

"Maybe he did," Zoe said.

Keira chuckled. "I don't think so. A big, white, furry guy? Sounds like a yeti, but I'm pretty sure they don't go around telling little boys to be quiet. Nah, he's just got Bigfoot on the brain. He's obsessed."

"I'm really sorry," Zoe said again.

"I know," Keira said. "I know you didn't mean for it to happen." She sighed. "I'm just glad everyone is okay."

Riley finished with the washcloth and Zoe stood. Her hands and knees were sore, along with her lip and brow. But overall, she was okay. "I think I'm going to go lie down as well."

"I'll come with."

"Don't be long," Keira said. "We've got to work on that Bronco."

"Right," Riley said.

Zoe led the way upstairs and Riley carefully helped her out of her dirty clothes and into fresh ones.

"You sure you don't want to shower? We have hot water again."

"Maybe after I nap." She just wanted to lie down and crash. Her poor heart was still hammering after the episode with Phoenix.

"Okay." Riley sat next her as she reclined.

"You gonna be all right?" Riley asked.

"Mm-hm." But her mind was back on that trail, chasing a phantom Phoenix. She'd probably have nightmares tonight. Dreams in which she couldn't find him.

"Hey, what is it? Everything turned out okay."

"It's just that…I don't know. I believe Phoenix. Something was out there, Riley."

"It was just his imagination." Riley stroked her face. "You know how kids are."

"Yes, but then how do you explain the dog then? She took off after something and just before they came running back, she barked at something that scared her. You should've heard that bark. It was—scary. And the way she's been barking here at night—"

"Okay, let's not get carried away," Riley said, cupping her cheek. "You're hurt and you're tired and you're on emotional overload. Just try to close your eyes and get some rest, okay? Everything turned out fine. There's nothing more to worry about."

"Riley, I'm being serious."

"And so am I. I think you've been worrying for so long that you don't know how to shut it off. It's like you've been in flight-or-fight mode for the better part of a year and your body doesn't know how to downshift from that."

Zoe didn't say anything. She couldn't argue with that. Riley was right.

But she was still concerned. Something wasn't right. She could feel it.

But she decided to humor her. She couldn't stand the look of worry on her beautiful face.

"Okay, I'll get some rest."

"Thank you." Riley placed a gentle kiss on her forehead, but it did little to comfort her.

CHAPTER FORTY-ONE

"And you believe her?" Keira asked as they worked under the hood of the Bronco.

"Yes, I believe her. What's not to believe? I mean look at what happened."

"Yes, a lot has happened, I'll give you that. But you gotta admit, her story sounds a little crazy. Come on, Ri, someone going to all this trouble over someone else? Who would do that? *Why* would they do that?"

"I don't know. People do weird shit. Especially when they get obsessed."

"It sounds crazy to me."

"Then how do you explain what happened? The busted generator, the cut wires, the dead hunter with all her stuff in his vehicle?"

Keira shook her head. "Maybe he was nutso. Maybe he saw you two and wanted to fuck with you. Doesn't mean he's been stalking her for over a year. I mean come on. He follows her up here in a snowstorm? And he *finds* her? Give me a break. No, he was just a crazy hunter who wanted to mess with you. And he got his so you have nothing more to worry about."

"That's what I told Zoe, but she's still anxious."

"See? Sounds like she's a bit of a drama queen, Ri. Something always has to be wrong."

Riley glanced over at her long-time friend. "I don't like you talking about her like that. She's not a drama queen. If anything she just wants peace. She just can't seem to find it. Something *is* always going wrong."

"Sounds like drama to me." Keira looked at her. "You can give me that look all you want, I'm still gonna say it. Someone has to look out for you."

"I can look out for myself, and I really like this woman, Keira, so please try and accept her. She's really nice and—"

"Okay, okay. Stop. I don't need the hard sell. I'll give her a chance. For your sake. But Elise is another story. After the whole Phoenix thing, good luck convincing her."

"That was an accident. Zoe couldn't help that."

"Yeah, well, you have to sell that to Elise, not me. And like I said, good luck."

"Jesus, I wish you guys would relax and give her a chance."

Keira looked at her again. "The sex is good, isn't it? I knew it. I knew it."

"Stop."

"It is, isn't it? No, it's better than good. That's why you're pushing so hard for us to give her a chance. She's hot in the sack and you're hopelessly smitten."

Riley shook her head but then slowly smiled. She couldn't help herself.

Keira slapped her knee. "I freaking knew it! Elise owes me a five-dollar bill."

"My sex life was only worth a five-dollar bet? Gosh, thanks, pal."

"Five bucks is good money. Besides, neither of us thought there'd ever be anything to bet about again. We thought you were going all nun on us."

"God, you two are a pain in the ass."

Keira laughed. "Yes, we are. And you love us."

"Unfortunately for me, I do indeed."

❖

"I wanna hold it," Phoenix said, trying to take the wire hanger with the marshmallow on the end.

"Phee, that's not how we ask," Keira said.

Phoenix sighed and looked at Riley with pleading eyes. "May I please hold it, Riley?"

Riley smiled and handed it over. "Yes, you may."

Phoenix eagerly took it and settled in in front of the fire. Then he waved Zoe over. "Come on, Zoe. Fire's toasty like toast." He giggled and Riley ruffled his hair.

She and Keira had finished the Bronco a few hours before and the gang had settled in playing games, telling stories and going for walks, without Shiloh, who had pouted profusely at the door.

"One more, Phoenix, and then it's bedtime," Elise said.

Phoenix's face crumpled. "I don't wanna go to bed, Mama!"

"Hey, little man," Keira said. "Why the fit over bedtime?"

Phoenix rarely wanted to go to bed, especially when they were making s'mores, but he'd never pitched a fit quite like this.

He lowered his marshmallow and began to cry. "Because of Bigfoot. He's gonna get me."

"Oh, come here, bud," Riley said, scooping him up. She handed his marshmallow to Zoe who looked empathetic.

"Bigfoot's not out there, sweetie," Keira said.

"He is, he is!"

He cried some more, trembling in Riley's arms. "Please don't make me go to bed," he said, clinging to Riley.

Keira stood and crossed to them. She took Phoenix from Riley and held him close, softly cooing to him.

"There, there, it's okay. You can sleep with Mamas tonight."

"But he'll get you, too."

"No, no he won't, love. Riley locks everything up real tight."

Just then Shiloh took off toward the back windows, barking loudly, tail held high, hackles raised.

"Jesus," Keira said, giving Riley a look.

"Shiloh, shush." Riley hurried to her and eased her away from the window.

Phoenix cried harder.

Riley took Shiloh to Zoe who calmed her further. But she still growled and her hackles were still raised.

"It's just elk, Phee," Riley said. "Shiloh barks at the elk every night. Come see."

Zoe held the dog while Keira took Phoenix to the back door. They couldn't see well in the dark, so Riley opened the door and stepped outside. "Shh, come on, come see."

They walked to the railing and looked down into the ravine. Riley turned on her flashlight and shined it down unto the trees and brush, expecting to see elk. But there was nothing at all.

Phoenix turned his face back into Keira's shoulder. "I don't wanna look."

"I could've sworn there'd be elk," Riley said. "Dog must've scared them away."

The back door opened and Elise came out and took Phoenix from Keira. "Say night night."

Phoenix refused, rubbing his face into his mother's shoulder.

"Night, Phee," Riley said.

"I'll be in in a sec," Keira said.

Zoe came out as Elise went in.

"Did you see the elk?" she asked.

"No. Shiloh must've scared them off."

"Don't elk usually graze at sundown and sunup?" Zoe asked.

Riley swept her light over the ravine again. Nothing.

"Yes, but—"

Zoe hugged herself. "She's barking at something else. I'm telling you, Riley, she is."

Keira placed a hand on Riley's shoulder as they walked back inside. She whispered, "Drama llama," in her ear just before they entered the house.

And for once, Riley wondered if she might be right.

CHAPTER FORTY-TWO

Zoe and Riley rose at dawn and quietly dressed. The night had been crazy, with Shiloh continuing to bark off and on, which kept waking Phoenix. Eventually, they'd had to carry the dog up the staircase to sleep with them. But sleep still hadn't been fast coming.

Zoe had tossed and turned, upset over the incident in the woods with Phoenix, concerned and disturbed by what he said he saw. Not to mention Shiloh's behavior. She just knew something was off. But Riley, surprisingly, had shut her down completely when she'd tried to talk about it. She'd said she was tired and didn't want to hear about it. That everything was just fine and that she needed to let things go.

Needless to say, they hadn't made love. They'd even slept facing away from one another. Zoe had felt just as cold and alone as she had her very first night on the mountain.

Now it was dawn and things didn't feel much warmer. Riley carried Shiloh down the stairs and the three of them opened the back door to step out onto the patio. Riley walked to the edge and smiled. She turned to Zoe and whispered, "Come here."

Zoe crept up to her and there, down in the ravine, were five elk grazing.

Shiloh trotted up to their pant legs, looked at the elk, sniffed the air, and then went off to do her business on the side of the house.

Zoe's heart sank. "She didn't react."

"I guess not. She barked herself to death last night. I think she's over them."

"No," Zoe said. "She should still show some interest."

"Zoe," Riley sighed.

"I'm serious, Riley. If she were so adamant to get to the elk, then why the hell is she acting like she couldn't care less now? I'm telling you she's not barking at elk. Something else is out there."

"Like what? Bigfoot?"

"Very funny."

"Well, what do you want me to say?"

"I want you to consider that I may be right. I was before."

"Right. But that's over, Zoe. Let it go. We're safe."

Zoe shook her head. "I think you're wrong, but I hope, for our sakes, you're right."

She walked back into the house, knowing darn well that Riley wasn't going to give in. She was once again, alone.

"Hey, you," Keira said as she opened the back door just as Zoe reached it. "Morning."

"Morning," Zoe said, not feeling the least bit chipper.

"Rough night, eh? Yeah, Phoenix was up nearly all night. Scared to death over Bigfoot."

"If it's any conciliation, I was too."

Keira's eyes widened as Zoe walked past her. She made her way into the kitchen where Elise was busy making Phoenix something to eat.

"Hi, Zoe," Phoenix said sadly from his position on the barstool.

"Hi, hon." She squeezed his shoulder as she walked to the coffee maker and poured herself a mug full.

"Good morning," she said to Elise after she took a long sip.

"Good morning." She was busy making Phoenix the Mickey Mouse waffles. She placed one on a plate, doused it in syrup, and cut it into small pieces before she served it to him. Then she walked to the table and sat down with her own mug of coffee. Zoe joined her.

"So, are you going to stay up here with Riley a bit longer?"

"Maybe a few days," Zoe said, hair already prickling at the questioning. "The sheriff's department did ask us to stick around while they investigate."

"Ah. Yeah, I guess they would. Is your job going to be okay with that?"

Zoe shifted. "I really don't know. I'm hoping they'll understand."

"Hard to say." She sipped her coffee and studied Zoe. "So what about Riley? Are you going to continue seeing her down in Phoenix?"

Zoe felt herself flush. "I don't know. I hope so."

"Riley's not one to play around."

Zoe wasn't sure what to say.

"Have you thought much about seeing her beyond this?"

"I—"

"Because I'd really hate to see Riley get hurt. So if you're not serious, you should end things now. End things before my friend gets hurt."

Zoe blinked at her. What was happening?

The back door opened, and Riley and Keira came walking in.

"Breakfast isn't ready?" Keira teased them.

"Mine is!" Phoenix said, raising his fork high in the air.

Riley laughed and hurried to him. "Did you save some for me? Huh?" He gave her a bite of his waffle and she danced. "Mm, mm so good. I'm gonna eat it all."

"Noo!"

Normally Zoe would warm at such a display of love and happiness, but at the moment she was thinking of nothing but Elise's words. She stood and excused herself from the table. Then she walked back outside with Shiloh. They were halfway down the side of the house when she heard Riley calling out for her.

"Hey, wait up." She hurried up to fall into step next to her. "What are you doing?"

"Going for a walk."

"Alone?"

"Yes."

"Why?"

"Because I'm not feeling very comfortable at the moment. Between you and your friends, I think I'm better off just walking down this mountain."

"Wait a minute." Riley gently cupped her arm. "What happened?"

"I just don't feel very welcome. You, once again, think I'm paranoid and Elise…"

"Elise what?"

"Elise told me I should end things with you now if I'm not serious."

"What?" Riley's face contorted in disbelief.

"She—kept asking about whether or not I've thought about our future and if I'm not serious I should end things now."

Riley clamped her mouth closed and breathed deeply. She shook her head. "She's got no right. No right."

"I think she's just looking out for you, but it made me feel really unwelcome and uncomfortable. I think I should just go."

"No," Riley said flatly. "Absolutely not."

"But, Riley, I'm the one causing all the problems. Phoenix, you, now your friends—"

"No, you're not going anywhere." She lightly tugged on her. "Come on, come back inside."

"Riley—"

"Please? We need to work this out."

"There's nothing to work out. Your friends want me gone and maybe they're right. I mean we have only just met and—"

"So, we spend time getting to know one another better. That's how relationships work. You don't just give up because your friends butt in. Come on, come back inside."

"I'm not going in there while you try to work this out with your friends. Talk about uncomfortable."

"Then you go inside with Shiloh and the rest of us will go for a walk."

Zoe considered it. Going for a walk all alone was the last thing she wanted to do, especially with how she'd been feeling about the mysterious dog barking and the incident with Phoenix.

"Okay," she said, causing Riley to smile.

"Thanks." She wrapped an arm around her. "You'll see, I'll get the whole thing sorted. Everything will be fine."

Zoe leaned into her and once again hoped she was right.

CHAPTER FORTY-THREE

Riley walked ahead of the group, stomped her boots at the door, and came back inside. Zoe was sitting in the chair by the fire, all curled up reading a paperback. She set it down when she saw Riley.

"What's wrong?"

Riley threw up her hands, so angry and frustrated she could scream.

"What's that mean?" Zoe asked.

But the door opened, and Phoenix came bounding in with his mothers close behind. If they looked anything like Riley, then it was no wonder Zoe had sensed something was going on.

Keira and Elise walked quietly through the kitchen back toward the hallway while Phoenix ambled up slowly to Zoe.

"I have to go now, Zoe," he said solemnly. "Mamas said we have stuff we need to do at home."

"Oh, no," Zoe said, hugging him tight. "I'm so sorry." She looked at Riley with tears in her eyes, questioning her with her wide gaze.

Riley shook her head and sank down onto the couch. She rested her elbows on her knees and ran her hands through her hair.

The talk had not gone well. For one thing, Phoenix was terrified to walk ahead, so he had stuck close to his mothers. So they'd had to talk in "code" for the majority of the conversation. But one thing had remained clear. Her friends did not approve of the fast track she was taking with Zoe. And they were concerned about her just up and leaving her job to escape up to the mountain and her sudden interest in sticking with Riley when she should be going home to return to her life like any normal person would do. Riley had tried to explain. They didn't understand all that Zoe had been through. But like it or not, her friends did have some good points. She just honestly didn't want to hear them. She knew how she felt about Zoe and that was all that mattered.

Keira called Phoenix into the bedroom.

"I gotta go," he said to Zoe and walked like a man condemned back through the kitchen.

"They're leaving?" Zoe asked softly. "Riley, no, I can't let that happen. I should be the one going."

Riley held up her hand to stop her without looking up.

"It's been decided. Just please let it happen."

"I should at least try to make amends. Something."

Riley sighed and looked up at her. She looked so beautiful and innocent sitting there all curled up with a book in her hand, firelight dancing upon her face.

"No, really. Just let it be."

Keira and Elise came back out with their luggage in tow. Phoenix brought up the rear with his dinosaur rolling suitcase.

Riley went to him and gently lifted his chin. "You can come back soon, bud. I promise."

"'K," he said, wiping a tear.

Riley enveloped him in a big hug and wiped a tear herself. Then she said her good-byes to Keira and Elise. Zoe said good-bye as well and the trio headed out the door, off to Riley's SUV. Riley stepped outside and waved as they drove off, leaving nothing but the silence and the whoosh of the wind in their wake.

Zoe joined her on the patio. "So, you'll be taking the Bronco home then?"

"Yes."

"But you were supposed to ride home with them, weren't you?"

"That was the original plan, yes. But things change."

"I'm sorry, Riley. I really am. I feel terrible—"

"Shh." Riley put her arm around her. "Let's go for a walk. What do you say? Take Shiloh and see if we can't find ourselves a Bigfoot."

Zoe laughed and slugged her in the arm. "You're an ass."

Riley smiled. "Maybe."

Zoe opened the back door, stepped into her boots, and called for Shiloh. The dog bounded outside with excitement and the three of them headed off on the same trail Zoe had taken with Phoenix the day before.

"This is where it happened?" Riley asked, keeping her eyes keen.

"Yes."

But they ended up seeing nothing. Nothing but the beauty of the forest around them.

They walked hand in hand for about an hour and then returned to the cabin where they cooked and ate breakfast. After that they napped and then relaxed and talked. By evening they were both reading, Zoe in the chair, Riley on the couch. The fire was burning down, and Riley rose to rouse it again but Zoe stopped her.

"No, don't. Let it be." She moved to the coffee table and lit two barrel candles, filling the dim room with flickering light. Then she tugged Riley back to the couch and pushed her down.

Riley grinned, liking the determined look on her face.

"What are you doing?"

"Whatever it is I want."

"Really? I like the sound of that."

Zoe crawled on top of her and took her book and tossed it onto to the floor.

"Easy, I'm liking that book," Riley said.

"You'll like this a whole lot better." Zoe held her face and kissed her hard and deep, causing Riley to groan with approval. Outside, the wind howled and a winter rain began to fall.

"Mm, you're right. I do like this a whole lot better."

"See, I told you." She drew back and stripped off her sweater. Then removed her bra.

Riley groaned again as she ran her hands along her silky torso.

"And you haven't seen nothing yet," Zoe said, arching back as Riley began playing with her nipples. But when she opened her eyes and leaned forward again to kiss her, her eyes widened and she screamed.

At first Riley thought she was caught up in the moment or in the pleasure, but then Zoe screamed again and bolted from Riley's arms. Completely shocked, Riley stood, tried to go to her, but Zoe was clamoring toward the fireplace, scrambling with her clothes.

And that's when Riley heard it. Heard what Zoe had seen that had scared the hell out of her.

A voice.

A man's voice.

From behind the couch.

CHAPTER FORTY-FOUR

Don't stop on account of me," the man said.

Zoe scooted as far back as she could go, heart hammering in her chest, until she hit the stone hearth. The dog barked, showing her teeth. Riley stood frozen by the couch, face ashen.

"You see, I'd wanted you all for myself, Zoe. But I have to admit the show was worth the price of admission."

He took a step closer and Riley backed away. Zoe struggled to cover herself, yanking on her sweater.

"Who are you?" Riley demanded.

The man, wearing white snow gear and a fur lined hood, merely cocked his head.

"Oh, you mean you don't recognize me, Zoe?" He laughed. "Well, let me fix that." He lowered his hood and revealed a sharply carved face with a prominent five o'clock shadow. His hair was dark, his eyes blue and piercing.

Zoe shook her head. "I don't understand."

His eyes narrowed as if her inability to recognize him had insulted him greatly.

"You mean you don't know who I am?"

Zoe shook her head again, trying to place him. He looked familiar, but not familiar enough.

"She doesn't know you, so you need to leave. Now," Riley said.

The man looked at her as if he were amused. Then he laughed a very sinister laugh. "I'm sorry, I find that very funny. You think you're in charge here." He reached in his coat and pulled out a gun. He aimed it at her.

"Care to continue? Dyke."

Riley inched backward, hands up.

"That's more like it," he said. Then he aimed the gun at Zoe. "Now, back to you." The dog barked again, and it hit Zoe that the man must've gained entry into the house when they'd gone for a walk with the dog.

"Somebody shut that dog up or I'll shoot it dead where it stands."

"No!" Zoe hugged the dog, shielding her with her body.

The man laughed again. "Zoe, Zoe, Zoe. Ever the animal lover. What am I going to do with you?" His eyes glimmered. "I know what I'd like to do with you. Especially after seeing your little performance." He grinned wickedly.

"Over my dead body," Riley let out, teeth clenched.

"That's not a bad idea." He aimed the gun at her again and this time pulled the trigger.

Riley fell backward and Zoe screamed and hurried to her.

"She was in the way," the man said, examining his gun as if it were a pesky hangnail. "Better to get rid of her now."

Zoe held her face and then pressed the wound in her shoulder. Riley was moaning, her eyes wide.

"Run, Zoe. Go. Just go."

Zoe shook her head. "I'm not leaving you."

"No one's going anywhere," the man said. "At least not yet."

He pointed the gun at Zoe. "Come on, get up."

"You just said we weren't leaving."

"Correct. We aren't going to leave the cabin. Not until we have to. But we are going to go into the bedroom, so I can get another peek at my prize."

"No," Zoe said. "I'm not going anywhere with you." She pressed harder on Riley's wound and felt the hot blood oozing through her fingers. The dog was on the other side of Riley, like another caregiver, licking her face.

Riley reached up, grabbed Zoe by the collar, pulled her down closer, and spoke. "The gun. In the curio."

Zoe blinked and stroked her cheek, letting her know she'd heard her.

She stood, ready to do what she had to do. Like it or not, this fight was going to be up to her. She was going to have to do this on her own.

And then, as if fate were listening, the door blew open and the candles on the coffee table went out.

Chapter Forty-five

The man cursed at the darkness and Zoe took full advantage. She scrambled to the right of the couch and darted straight back toward the curio. But the man's eyes seemed to have adjusted just in time, because he lunged for her and tackled her into the curio cabinet, causing many of the contents to fall onto the floor.

Zoe cried out in pain and then fought in anger and terror. She had no choice but to go for his face, as his heavy coat covered most of his body. So she scratched and clawed, desperate to get to his eyes.

"Leave—me—alone!" she screamed. It couldn't end like this. It couldn't. He couldn't win. She'd been through too much.

He hissed with pain as her fingernails found their mark on his cheeks. Then he laughed.

"Yes, fight. I like a fighter. The harder the fight the harder I get."

She screamed and fought to claw his face again, but he caught her wrists and pinned her down.

She could smell his breath. It smelled like cigarettes and something rancid, along with his body odor. Like he hadn't bathed in days.

"Who—are you?"

He drew back, as if alarmed. "What do you mean? Do you really not know me?"

"No."

"Tenth grade? Ring a bell?"

She shook her head.

He hissed again, this time in disbelief and anger. "We went out. You and me."

She blinked rapidly, trying to focus more on his dim face. And then it hit her.

"Tom? Tom Malcott?"

He pushed upward and sat straddling her waist.

"In the flesh."

"But I don't understand. We—dated. That's all."

"Oh no, that's not all. We dated. For six months. We were in love. I wanted to marry you. I—"

"Tom, we were kids."

"I wrote you poetry, dreamt of our future, and you just up and dumped me. You never really loved me at all."

"We were kids. We were young. That's all."

"I was crushed," he said. "Depressed. You ruined my life."

She stared in disbelief. "I ruined your life? How?"

"Don't act like you don't know."

"I don't. I swear." She had no idea what he was talking about, but as long as he was talking he wasn't hurting her.

"After you dumped me my life turned to shit. I got in a bad fight because of you. With some senior. He was saying things about you and I didn't like it. So I broke his jaw and I got suspended. And then my mother made me move. To Maine. Where my uncle beat the shit out of me, day in and day out."

She was trying hard to compute all that he was saying.

"I do remember you leaving school, but—"

"Didn't bother to find out why? Well, that's why. The school wanted to keep the whole thing quiet. My mom paid the kid's medical bills and it was swept under the rug as long as I agreed to leave. Otherwise it would've been juvie for me."

But what the hell does this have to do with me?

She kept quiet and tried to sound soft and caring.

"I'm sorry that happened to you, Tom. It's terrible."

"Yeah, no thanks to you. You wouldn't even talk to me on the phone."

"I—we were—I'm sorry. I'm sorry, Tom. I really am."

"Sometimes sorry isn't good enough."

She hurried to speak before he could attack again. "If you've been so hurt by me, why did you wait so long to come after me?"

He rubbed his scruffy jaw as if he was thinking. But she didn't dare move, his weight still too much for her. She just remained quiet and listened.

"I had decided to let it go. Until you walked into my dealership to finance a car. I took one look at you and knew. You, on the other hand, obviously had no clue who I was. Figures. Still your selfish self."

Oh my God. The dealership. That's it. That's how he got all my info.

She wanted to point out that the last time she'd seen him he was all of five foot eight and scrawny for his age, but she didn't.

"I was stressed about buying a car. Why didn't you just say something?"

"Like what?" he shouted. "I had a job to do and you were just self-centered and selfish like always. So that's when I decided to make you pay. To take you and make you mine once and for all. Even if only for a night." He laughed. "Thanks to that little storm, it seems I'll get my wish, doesn't it?"

"Over my dead body." Riley's voice came from behind. There was a sickening thud and Tom fell off of her, cursing. Riley lifted what appeared to be the fire poker and hit him again. But his coat was so heavy it seemed to do very little damage. He managed to struggle to his feet and rush at Riley. Next to them the dog barked and Zoe tried to get to her feet, but her head was killing her and she was dizzy. Broken glass surrounded her, piercing into her palms as she fumbled around for the gun.

Please let it be down here.

She could hear Riley and Tom and the dog all wrestling around on the floor.

"Riley, I'm coming," she said. "I'm coming, Riley."

Hang on. I'm trying.

She searched desperately, feeling along the sharp bits of broken ceramic and glass, feeling tiny puncture wounds in her hands as she did so.

"Zoe," Riley croaked and Tom laughed.

"Fucking dyke."

He stood and spit as the dog whined. Then he held what looked like the fire poker over his head and brought it down on Riley.

"Nooooooo!" Zoe shouted, sitting up.

He turned on her and came at her. "What's the matter? Did I hurt your little girlfriend? I never pegged you for a dyke, Zoe."

He inhaled sharply through his nose making an awful noise and then spit again, this time toward her.

"But I guess I shoulda figured. Since you didn't want me and all."

Zoe clenched her jaw. "I didn't want you then and I don't want you now. Understand? I will NEVER want you, Tom. Do you HEAR me? I don't want you!"

"Fine, bitch, have it your way." He raised the poker above his head and just as he was bringing it down, Zoe found the gun down near her knee. She lifted it quickly and closed her eyes as she pulled the trigger, praying Riley had left it loaded.

She had.

The gunshot cracked and she opened her eyes to see Tom stumble, grabbing the right side of his chest. She fired again and hit the left side.

He looked at her and said, "Bitch," one last time before she fired the last shot, this one sending him falling backward.

Shiloh whined and came to her, and she scrambled for her feet and hurried to Riley. She was bleeding from her shoulder, from the bullet wound and from a small place on her ribs.

She moaned as Zoe cradled her head.

"Hang on, Riley, hang on."

She glanced around the dim cabin, trying to figure out what to do. Then she looked at Tom, lying in a heap on the floor.

He had to have gotten here somehow. And I bet his how is not far away.

She compressed Riley's wounds as best she could and crawled to Tom. She felt his pulse and found none. Then she checked his pockets. She found his gun and his car keys.

Bingo.

"Come on, girl," she said to Shiloh. "We gotta go find a vehicle."

She stepped into her boots and slid on her coat and stepped out into the frigid cold rain. Then she searched for tracks and headed out, praying all along that Riley would be able to hang on.

CHAPTER FORTY-SIX

R iley opened her eyes and immediately regretted it. The sun was shining fully and beaming in right through the floor-to-ceiling windows, biting into her eyes. She moaned a little as she tried to push herself up.

"No, no, no. Don't do that." It was Elise and she was rushing to her, trying to get her to stop. "Just lie still." She eased Riley back down and Riley had the urge to close her eyes again. She did so, but she fought sleep, which was very difficult to do.

"There, just relax and rest." She smoothed her hair back, lulling her back to dreamland. Riley almost climbed aboard the ship that would take her there, the press of the warm fire encouraging her, along with the crackling of the logs.

I'm home, in the cabin. I'm safe.

She was just about to fall asleep when she remembered.

The man.

Zoe.

Gunshots.

The hospital.

Oh, God.

Her eyes flew open and she panicked, trying once again to sit up.

"Riley, no!" Elise pressed her back down once again. "You're still hurt."

"Zoe," Riley croaked. "Where—"

Elise closed her mouth with the press of her finger. "Zoe's fine, remember?"

"Where—"

"You'll see her soon enough."

"No, now."

"Riley, you need to rest."

"No." Riley groaned in agony as she pushed herself up. Her friends didn't like Zoe. They didn't understand. They were probably keeping Zoe from her.

"What's going on?" Keira asked as she came into the room, holding Phoenix's hand.

"Wow, Riley Robinson is awake!" He released Kiera's hand to bound to her, but Elise caught him just before he pounced on her.

"You can't jump on her, love. She's injured, remember?"

"Oh."

"Hey, bud, I'm okay," Riley said with a raspy voice.

I think.

She glanced down at herself.

She saw the bandaging on her shoulder, felt more along her ribs.

Oh, right. I was shot and beaten. Spent a couple of days in the hospital. How could I forget?

It just made her curiosity about Zoe all the stronger, because she'd yet to see her.

But before she could ask again, there was a knock at the door and a shriek of excitement and glee from Phoenix.

"Zoe!" He leapt from the couch to the back door where Keira met him to open it.

Riley couldn't totally see Zoe from her position, but her heart was pounding, both in anticipation and fear. How would her friends respond? What all had happened after the hospital? She could remember very little.

Phoenix shrieked again as the door opened and he greeted the dog.

"Shiloh! Look, it's Shiloh!"

The beautiful white husky that had bonded with her and Zoe came trotting in and Phoenix was once again in heaven.

"She's white like snow," Phoenix said, delighted.

Shiloh hurried over to her and placed her head in her lap.

"Hiya, girl," Riley said, thrilled to see her. "I had wondered what happened to you."

Then Zoe stepped into the room, and to Riley's further surprise she saw another dog, this one in her arms. It was a small white terrier mix. Phoenix caught sight of it and about lost his mind.

"Another doggie! Look, Mamas, she brought two!"

Zoe knelt with the dog and smiled at Phoenix. "That's right. I've got two dogs now. The big one is Shiloh and the little one is Annie."

She allowed Phoenix to pet Annie, all the while smiling softly at him. And then her eyes settled on Riley's and Riley's entire body warmed. She looked so incredibly beautiful in the firelight with her whiskey eyes and chestnut hair. So vibrant and alive. And so...free.

"You look amazing," Riley said through a clenched throat.

Zoe stood and carefully knelt next to her.

"A real sight for sore eyes."

Zoe blushed. "It's good to see you, too. Really good. I've been so worried." She reached up and touched her face. "So good to see that you're okay now. I was so worried that first day in the hospital. You were so out of it."

"You were there?"

"Of course. But only for the first day." She patted her hand.

"Come on, Phee, let's take the dogs for a walk," Keira said.

She hooked the dogs up to their leashes and Riley mouthed a silent thank you to them before they left. Keira and Elise had merely smiled in return.

The cabin fell silent as they closed the door behind them, leaving Riley and Zoe all alone.

"What actually happened?" Riley asked.

"What do you remember?"

"Not much after being shot and beaten. I can recall some of the hospital stay. Are you—okay?" She choked up at the thought of her having been injured. "Did he—hurt you?"

Zoe quickly shook her head. "Not like that, no. We fought some, he tackled me into the curio cabinet, and I got some scrapes and bruises. But nothing like you."

"Is he—alive?"

"No. I shot him."

Riley swallowed. *Jesus.*

"And then I found his SUV down the road a ways and I drove you into town for help. And that's where I found Annie. She was in the SUV. Poor thing was all alone and cold."

"You mean she's *his* dog?"

"I guess so. Cops told me he had recently adopted her and apparently used her as a decoy when he stalked my house."

"Seriously?"

"Yes, my neighbor's doorbell camera shows it all."

"So you're keeping her?"

"Sure am. She's sweet. And it's not her fault he was a psycho. Besides, she kept a close eye on you on the way into town." Zoe winked.

"And Annie and Shiloh get along?"

"Like two peas in a pod."

Zoe held her hand and kissed it. "Kind of like us."

"Speaking of us," Riley said. "Are Keira and Elise being nice to you?"

"They know the whole story now, and they know how much I care about you."

"Does everyone know the whole story but me?"

Zoe smiled. "All you need to know is that an old high school boyfriend of mine helped me finance a new car and then he went nuts on me."

"But you didn't recognize him."

Zoe laughed. "No. My God, it's been years and he was very small last time I saw him. And honestly, he wasn't a good memory to have. He kind of scared me a little. Even back then."

"So why did he come after you? Did he say?"

"Because I ruined his life by breaking up with him. He got into a lot of trouble shortly thereafter and blamed me for it."

"So, what, you were like always on his hit list or something?"

"I guess so."

"What a crazy bastard."

"I wasn't the only woman either. There have been others."

"You're kidding."

Zoe shook her head. "One woman he actually sexually assaulted after breaking into her home at night. They'd never caught him. But the idiot left evidence of it in his home. Left evidence of all his victims. If only the police had suspected him sooner and searched his home."

"Would've saved you a whole lot of trouble."

"Yes."

"What about the hunter?"

Zoe sighed. "Apparently, he was just a guy wanting to get away to his friend's cabin. He'd planned on hunting, but of course, the storm stopped him."

"Why did he have your stuff?"

"The sheriff's department said he'd found it and collected it to bring it down to show them. I guess he'd left a note at his friend's cabin describing a drifter, a man he had seen around. Said he was going to try to make it back down the mountain after a rough run-in with him."

"Wow," Riley said, amazed. "So, he'd seen the guy. Interacted with him."

"Yes, and he'd thought my stuff belonged to him."

Riley touched her face, so grateful everything turned out okay. "Thank God you're okay. Thank God."

"*We're* okay," she corrected her. "Thank God *we're* okay."

"So what's the plan now?" Riley asked, wanting more than anything to kiss her.

"The plan now is to get you healthy. Keira and Elise need to get back home for the week so I said I'd come stay with you."

"Here, in the cabin?"

"Couldn't think of a better place." She smiled. "I took a much needed leave of absence from my job after I first visited you in the hospital. That's where I was. Back home in Phoenix getting things settled so I could come back here and care for you."

"You mean you aren't afraid? To be here?"

"Now? Hell no. Besides, I know where that gun is should we need it."

"I think the cops probably have the gun," Riley said.

Zoe shrugged. "Good, we don't need it anyway."

She leaned in and kissed Riley softly on the lips. "We've got each other."

Riley moaned as she kissed her back. "That we do. That we do."

They kissed until Phoenix came bouncing back in, requesting to watch *The Wizard of Oz.* Then they all settled in, popped some popcorn, and watched the movie.

And Riley felt the best she'd ever felt, surrounded by those she loved most.

THE END

About the Author

An avid reader from early childhood, Ronica Black spends a great deal of time with her nose in a book, whether that be one she's working on herself or another author's. When she's not reading or writing, she's spending time with her little rescue dog, Frankie, hiking, or exploring the great state of Arizona with friends. She also enjoys painting, drawing, and doing anything creative. She lives in the greater Phoenix area.

Books Available from Bold Strokes Books

Boy at the Window by Lauren Melissa Ellzey. Daniel Kim struggles to hold onto reality while haunted by both his very-present past and his never-present parents. Jiwon Yoon may be the only one who can break Daniel free. (978-1-63679-092-3)

Deadly Secrets by VK Powell. Corporate criminals want whistleblower Jana Elliott permanently silenced, but Rafe Silva will risk everything to keep the woman she loves safe. (978-1-63679-087-9)

Enchanted Autumn by Ursula Klein. When Elizabeth comes to Salem, Massachusetts, to study the witch trials, she never expects to find love—or an actual witch…and Hazel might just turn out to be both. (978-1-63679-104-3)

Escorted by Renee Roman. When fantasy meets reality, will escort Ryan Lewis be able to walk away from a chance at forever with her new client Dani? (978-1-63679-039-8)

Her Heart's Desire by Anne Shade. Two women. One choice. Will Eve and Lynette be able to overcome their doubts and fears to embrace their deepest desire? (978-1-63679-102-9)

My Secret Valentine by Julie Cannon, Erin Dutton, & Anne Shade. Winning the heart of your secret Valentine? These award-winning authors agree, there is no better way to fall in love. (978-1-63679-071-8)

Perilous Obsession by Carsen Taite. When reporter Macy Moran becomes consumed with solving a cold case, will her quest for the truth bring her closer to Detective Beck Ramsey or will her obsession with finding a murderer rob her of a chance at true love? (978-1-63679-009-1)

Reading Her by Amanda Radley. Lauren and Allegra learn love and happiness are right where they least expect it. There's just one problem: Lauren has a secret she cannot tell anyone, and Allegra knows she's hiding something. (978-1-63679-075-6)

The Willing by Lyn Hemphill. Kitty Wilson doesn't know how, but she can bring people back from the dead as long as someone is willing to take their place and keep the universe in balance. (978-1-63679-083-1)

Three Left Turns to Nowhere by Nathan Burgoine, J. Marshall Freeman, & Jeffrey Ricker. Three strangers heading to a convention in Toronto are stranded in rural Ontario, where a small town with a subtle kind of magic leads each to discover what he's been searching for. (978-1-63679-050-3)

Watching Over Her by Ronica Black. As they face the snowstorm of the century, and the looming threat of a stalker, Riley and Zoey just might find love in the most unexpected of places. (978-1-63679-100-5)

#shedeservedit by Greg Herren. When his gay best friend, and high school football star, is murdered, Alex Wheeler is a suspect and must find the truth to clear himself. (978-1-63555-996-5)

Always by Kris Bryant. When a pushy American private investigator shows up demanding to meet the woman in Camila's artwork, instead of introducing her to her great-grandmother, Camila decides to lead her on a wild goose chase all over Italy. (978-1-63679-027-5)

Exes and O's by Joy Argento. Ali and Madison really only have one thing in common. The girl who broke their heart may be the only one who can put it back together. (978-1-63679-017-6)

One Verse Multi by Sander Santiago. Life was good: promotion, friends, falling in love, discovering that the multi-verse is on a fast track to collision—wait, what? Good thing Martin King works for a company that can fix the problem, right…um…right? (978-1-63679-069-5)

Paris Rules by Jaime Maddox. Carly Becker has been searching for the perfect woman all her life, but no one ever seems to be just right until Paige Waterford checks all her boxes, except the most important one—she's married. (978-1-63679-077-0)

Shadow Dancers by Suzie Clarke. In this third and final book in the Moon Shadow series, Rachel must find a way to become the hunter and not the hunted, and this time she will meet Ehsee Yumiko head-on. (978-1-63555-829-6)

The Kiss by C.A. Popovich. When her wife refuses their divorce and begins to stalk her, threatening her life, Kate realizes to protect her new love, Leslie, she has to let her go, even if it breaks her heart. (978-1-63679-079-4)

The Wedding Setup by Charlotte Greene. When Ryann, a big-time New York executive, goes to Colorado to help out with her best friend's wedding, she never expects to fall for the maid of honor. (978-1-63679-033-6)

Velocity by Gun Brooke. Holly and Claire work toward an uncertain future preparing for an alien space mission, and only one thing is for certain, they will have to risk their lives, and their hearts, to discover the truth. (978-1-63555-983-5)

Wildflower Words by Sam Ledel. Lida Jones treks West with her father in search of a better life on the rapidly developing American frontier, but finds home when she meets Hazel Thompson. (978-1-63679-055-8)

A Fairer Tomorrow by Kathleen Knowles. For Maddie Weeks and Gerry Stern, the Second World War brought them together, but the end of the war might rip them apart. (978-1-63555-874-6)

Holiday Hearts by Diana Day-Admire and Lyn Cole. Opposites attract during Christmastime chaos in Kansas City. (978-1-63679-128-9)

Changing Majors by Ana Hartnett Reichardt. Beyond a love, beyond a coming-out, Bailey Sullivan discovers what lies beyond the shame and self-doubt imposed on her by traditional Southern ideals. (978-1-63679-081-7)

Fresh Grave in Grand Canyon by Lee Patton. The age-old Grand Canyon becomes more and more ominous as a group of volunteers fight to survive alone in nature and uncover a murderer among them. (978-1-63679-047-3)

Highland Whirl by Anna Larner. Opposites attract in the Scottish Highlands, when feisty Alice Campbell falls for city-girl-about-town Roxanne Barns. (978-1-63555-892-0)

Humbug by Amanda Radley. With the corporate Christmas party in jeopardy, CEO Rosalind Caldwell hires Christmas Girl Ellie Pearce as her personal assistant. The only problem is, Ellie isn't a PA, has never planned a party, and develops a ridiculous crush on her totally intimidating new boss. (978-1-63555-965-1)

On the Rocks by Georgia Beers. Schoolteacher Vanessa Martini makes no apologies for her dating checklist, and newly single mom Grace Chapman ticks all Vanessa's Do Not Date boxes. Of course, they're never going to fall in love. (978-1-63555-989-7)

Song of Serenity by Brey Willows. Arguing with the Muse of music and justice is complicated, falling in love with her even more so. (978-1-63679-015-2)

The Christmas Proposal by Lisa Moreau. Stranded together in a Christmas village on a snowy mountain, Grace and Bridget face their past and question their dreams for the future. (978-1-63555-648-3)

The Infinite Summer by Morgan Lee Miller. While spending the summer with her dad in a small beach town, Remi Brenner falls for Harper Hebert and accidentally finds herself tangled up in an intense restaurant rivalry between her famous stepmom and her first love. (978-1-63555-969-9)

Wisdom by Jesse J. Thoma. When Sophia and Reggie are chosen for the governor's new community design team and tasked with tackling substance abuse and mental health issues, battle lines are drawn even as sparks fly. (978-1-63555-886-9)

A Convenient Arrangement by Aurora Rey and Jaime Clevenger. Cuffing season has come for lesbians, and for Jess Archer and Cody Dawson, their convenient arrangement becomes anything but. (978-1-63555-818-0)

An Alaskan Wedding by Nance Sparks. The last thing either Andrea or Riley expects is to bump into the one who broke her heart fifteen years ago, but when they meet at the welcome party, their feelings come rushing back. (978-1-63679-053-4)

Beulah Lodge by Cathy Dunnell. It's 1874, and newly engaged Ruth Mallowes is set on marriage and life as a missionary... until she falls in love with the housemaid at Beulah Lodge. (978-1-63679-007-7)

Gia's Gems by Toni Logan. When Lindsey Speyer discovers that popular travel columnist Gia Williams is a complete fake and threatens to expose her, blackmail has never been so sexy. (978-1-63555-917-0)

Holiday Wishes & Mistletoe Kisses by M. Ullrich. Four holidays, four couples, four chances to make their wishes come true. (978-1-63555-760-2)

Love By Proxy by Dena Blake. Tess has a secret crush on her best friend, Sophie, so the last thing she wants is to help Sophie fall in love with someone else, but how can she stand in the way of her happiness? (978-1-63555-973-6)

Loyalty, Love, & Vermouth by Eric Peterson. A comic valentine to a gay man's family of choice, including the ones with cold noses and four paws. (978-1-63555-997-2)

Marry Me by Melissa Brayden. Allison Hale attempts to plan the wedding of the century to a man who could save her family's business, if only she wasn't falling for her wedding planner, Megan Kinkaid. (978-1-63555-932-3)

Pathway to Love by Radclyffe. Courtney Valentine is looking for a woman exactly like Ben—smart, sexy, and not in the market for anything serious. All she has to do is convince Ben that sex-without-strings is the perfect pathway to pleasure. (978-1-63679-110-4)

Sweet Surprise by Jenny Frame. Flora and Mac never thought they'd ever see each other again, but when Mac opens up her barber shop right next to Flora's sweet shop, their connection comes roaring back. (978-1-63679-001-5)

The Edge of Yesterday by CJ Birch. Easton Gray is sent from the future to save humanity from technological disaster. When she's forced to target the woman she's falling in love with, can Easton do what's needed to save humanity? (978-1-63679-025-1)

The Scout and the Scoundrel by Barbara Ann Wright. With unexpected danger surrounding them, Zara and Roni are stuck between duty and survival, with little room for exploring their feelings, especially love. (978-1-63555-978-1)

Bury Me in Shadows by Greg Herren. College student Jake Chapman is forced to spend the summer at his dying grandmother's home and soon finds danger from long-buried family secrets. (978-1-63555-993-4)

Can't Leave Love by Kimberly Cooper Griffin. Sophia and Pru have no intention of falling in love, but sometimes love happens when and where you least expect it. (978-1-636790041-1)

Free Fall at Angel Creek by Julie Tizard. Detective Dee Rawlings and aircraft accident investigator Dr. River Dawson use conflicting methods to find answers when a plane goes missing, while overcoming surprising threats, and discovering an unlikely chance at love. (978-1-63555-884-5)

Love's Compromise by Cass Sellars. For Piper Holthaus and Brook Myers, will professional dreams and past baggage stop two hearts from realizing they are meant for each other? (978-1-63555-942-2)

Not All a Dream by Sophia Kell Hagin. Hester has lost the woman she loved and the world has descended into relentless dark and cold. But giving up will have to wait when she stumbles upon people who help her survive. (978-1-63679-067-1)

Protecting the Lady by Amanda Radley. If Eve Webb had known she'd be protecting royalty, she'd never have taken the job as bodyguard, but as the threat to Lady Katherine's life draws closer, she'll do whatever it takes to save her, and may just lose her heart in the process. (978-1-63679-003-9)

The Secrets of Willowra by Kadyan. A family saga of three women, their homestead called Willowra in the Australian outback, and the secrets that link them all. (978-1-63679-064-0)

Trial by Fire by Carsen Taite. When prosecutor Lennox Roy and public defender Wren Bishop become fierce adversaries in a headline-grabbing arson case, their attraction ignites a passion that leads them both to question their assumptions about the law, the truth, and each other. (978-1-63555-860-9)

Turbulent Waves by Ali Vali. Kai Merlin and Vivien Palmer plan their future together as hostile forces make their own plans to destroy what they have, as well as all those they love. (978-1-63679-011-4)

Unbreakable by Cari Hunter. When Dr. Grace Kendal is forced at gunpoint to help an injured woman, she is dragged into a nightmare where nothing is quite as it seems, and their lives aren't the only ones on the line. (978-1-63555-961-3)

Veterinary Surgeon by Nancy Wheelton. When dangerous drugs are stolen from the veterinary clinic, Mitch investigates and Kay becomes a suspect. As pride and professions clash, love seems impossible. (978-1-63679-043-5)